A BOY AND A BEAR

"Listen," said Bart, Jason's friend and teammate, "is this stuff true? You can tell me."

"What stuff?"

"You know what stuff," Bart said. "The polar bear stuff."

Jason looked his friend in the eyes. He'd kept his relationship with Whitney a secret because he was afraid Bart would think it was strange. But now he felt bad that he hadn't shared it. If he couldn't trust Bart, who could he trust?

"Yeah," Jason said. "It's true. It's really no big deal. One day I was practicing my swing in the zoo courtyard. The next thing I knew, I heard a voice say 'Put 'a little more weight on your back foot. Snap your wrists more.' I looked up and there was Whitney. Since then, we've been good friends. . . ."

Jason and the Baseball Bear

by DAN ELISH

BANTAM BOOKS
NEW YORK · TORONTO · LONDON · SYDNEY · AUCKLAND

This edition contains the complete text
of the original hardcover edition.
NOT ONE WORD HAS BEEN OMITTED.

RL 4, 007–011

JASON AND THE BASEBALL BEAR

A Bantam Skylark Book / published by arrangement
with Orchard Books, a division of Franklin Watts, Inc.

PRINTING HISTORY
Orchard Books edition published 1990
Bantam edition / April 1992

Skylark Books is a registered trademark of Bantam Books,
a division of Bantam Doubleday Dell Publishing Group, Inc.
Registered in U.S. Patent and Trademark Office and elsewhere.

ISBN 0-553-15878-3

Published simultaneously in the United States and Canada

Bantam Books are published by Bantam Books, a division of Bantam
Doubleday Dell Publishing Group, Inc. Its trademark, consisting of the
words "Bantam Books" and the portrayal of a rooster, is Registered in
U.S. Patent and Trademark Office and in other countries. Marca
Registrada. Bantam Books, 666 Fifth Avenue, New York, New York 10103.

PRINTED IN THE UNITED STATES OF AMERICA

CWO   0 9 8 7 6 5 4 3 2 1

For Madeleine and Andy

Cast of Characters

Main Players

JASON—the only fourth grader on the Apaches.
The first ever to be able to talk to animals
DR. MUNSON—Jason's father, a psychiatrist
MRS. MUNSON—Jason's mother, a lawyer
JUDGE WARRINER—a judge at City Court, fan
of the old-time Brooklyn Dodgers
APACHE FANS—the hot dog man, the piano
tuner, the barber
HIGHLANDER FANS—the sergeant,
the orthodontist

The Animals

WHITNEY—an elderly polar bear. Jason's best
friend and a baseball genius
THE GNU—a Shakespearian scholar with an
English accent
THE PYTHON—a twenty-foot snake with
a prominent hiss
THE GORILLA—a large ape with a
mighty throwing arm
THE LIONESS—a gentle cat

The Apaches

MR. RICHARDSON
coach

WYATT TORPLE
center field

JIM LANIER
right field

KAREN WEBSTER
left field

WENDIE PHILLIPS
third base

SHORTY RODGERS
shortstop

JEREMY ATWATER
second base

JOHN KESSLER
first base

JUDY WHEELER
catcher

BART WAGNER
pitcher,
Jason's best
(human) friend

SUSAN O'CONNELL
reserve

FRANK KLAUS
reserve

The Highlanders

MR. O'MALLEY
coach

HOMER WIGGINS
center field

BOBBY WINDMEYER
right field

RAY THOMAS
left field

ERIC HADDEN
third base

ANNIE GREGORY
shortstop

NICK HANNING
second base

NINA SPINE
first base

JOSH ZIMMERMAN
catcher

JOEY FLANNIGAN
pitcher

JASON
AND THE
BASEBALL BEAR

①

THE minute Little League practice was over, Jason Munson jumped on his bike and pedaled as fast as he could toward the zoo. He cut into the park just below Maple Street, angling around the red brick Parks Department building, then up a steep hill and through a tall iron gate, and, finally, he was there.

"Hiya, Jason," Mr. Handy, the zookeeper, called.

"Hi," Jason said, stopping his bike past the entrance. "I'm going to see Whitney."

"Of course," Mr. Handy replied with a nod. "I'll let you know when I'm ready to lock up."

"Thanks," Jason said. "See you then."

Mr. Handy always let him visit Whitney and the others—even after public visiting hours were over. Jason rode on around the bird house, and skidded to a halt in front of Whitney's cage.

The elderly polar bear was browsing through the

afternoon's sports section. He turned each page carefully, nudging the edges of the paper with his big white paws and looking closely at the pictures, pressing his nose into the words, his brow wrinkled in concentration.

"Hi!" Jason said.

Whitney looked up. Seeing Jason, he smiled. His whiskers twitched; his whole being took on a glow.

"Hi there, young fella," he said, pushing the paper aside and leaning forward. "Ready for that first play-off game?"

"I think so," said Jason, a substitute infielder for the Apaches.

Whitney raised an eyebrow.

"What do you mean, you *think* so?"

"I mean I think we're gonna beat the Highlanders, but I don't know if I'm gonna play much."

"Don't say that," Whitney said, standing up on all fours. "You never know what's going to happen in the course of a play-off. Just remember all the things I've taught you, and when your turn comes you'll do just fine. Remember—a key hit can win a ball game."

"Like Bill Mazeroski's home run in the 1960 World Series," Jason said.

"Exactly! That hit won it for the Pittsburgh Pirates. But you've always got to be ready! And when you get up to the plate you've got to concentrate on that ball. Now let's see a few cuts—get your bat."

Jason grabbed it from his bike rack and squared off as if he were waiting for a pitch.

"Right!" Whitney said. "Good. Left elbow in . . . feet spread about a foot apart . . . concentrate on the pitcher . . . try to guess what he's gonna throw."

Jason whipped the bat around, hitting an imaginary ball.

"Looking good," Whitney said. "But keep that right elbow up. And have fun up there. That's right! Have confidence in yourself. You can hit! You know you can!"

Jason took another hard cut at the air.

"It's a triple down the right field line!" Whitney cried. "You look like Darryl Strawberry!"

"Thanks," Jason said, feeling himself blush. He looked around embarrassedly.

Whitney's cage was one of five that faced a cement courtyard in the zoo. In the cage to his right lived a lioness. In the two cages to his left were a gorilla and a twenty-foot python. Directly across the way was a gnu.

"Cheerio, Jason," the gnu called in a bright British accent. (The gnu had spent most of his life in the London Zoo. He was visiting America on an exchange program.) "As usual it's so very fine to see you."

Jason smiled.

"Tomorrow's the big baseball match, is it not?" the gnu continued.

"That's right," Jason said.

"Ahhh, baseball!" the gnu exclaimed. "Such a charming pastime. I wish I had the chance to learn more about it, but I'm bogged down right now re-reading the complete works of William Shake-speare."

"That's a lot of reading?" Jason asked.

"Yes! Yes!" the gnu said. "Thirty-six plays, not to mention the sonnets. But all entirely worth the ef-fort! Shakespeare was a master dramatist—an in-spired blender of meter, rhyme, and meaning."

Just then there was a hiss from the python, who was wrapping all twenty feet of himself around the tree in his cage.

"Did he ever write about bassseball?" the python asked, winking at Jason. "He couldn't have been sssuch a great writer if he overlooked bassseball."

"But baseball wasn't even invented when Shake-speare was alive," Jason said.

"That's correct!" the gnu cried. "But Shakespeare knew it was coming!"

"How'sss that?"

"Well, python, old fellow," the gnu continued. "Look at the opening of his play *Macbeth*. The set-ting is the middle of a dark and scary wood. Out of the mist, three witches appear and say: 'Fair is foul and foul is fair'!"

"So?" Jason asked.

"Don't you see!" the gnu exclaimed. "Obviously,

4

these witches represent umpires, debating whether or not baseball should have any foul territory!"

Before the python or Jason could respond to the gnu's theory, a shadow fell across the courtyard. The gorilla had come to the edge of his cage.

"Jason!" he boomed.

Only a few weeks earlier, the gorilla had been living wild in the jungle. He was finding it difficult to learn speech.

"Hiya!" Jason said. "How are you today?"

The gorilla appeared to ignore the question and turned his massive body to face the gnu.

"Goat! Goat! Goat!" he bellowed.

The gnu shook his head.

"No, no, no," he said. "I'm a gnu! A gnu! Not a goat. Goats are unsavory, gnus are elegant."

The gorilla swung back to Jason and began shaking the cage's bars.

"Jason hitty! Jason hitty!" he screamed.

"He must be wishing you luck tomorrow," Whitney said.

The gorilla extended his large hand and patted Jason on the head.

"Thanks, gorilla," Jason said. "But you know, I probably won't even play."

"Will you stop talking nonsense!" said a voice from the other side of the courtyard: the lioness. Jason looked at the sleek cat pacing back and forth in her cage. "You'll play, and even if you don't," she continued, "you shouldn't worry about it. Just remember—you're the *only* fourth grader on any Little League team in this city. That's quite an achievement in and of itself!"

The other animals nodded.

"Ye*sss* it i*sss*," the python said.

"Jason young!" the gorilla boomed.

"You've got plenty of time," Whitney agreed, wagging his big white head up and down. "Why, I read just the other day that Wade Boggs spent six years in the minor leagues before he was brought up to the majors."

"Really?" Jason asked.

"That's right," the bear replied.

Just then the gnu cleared his throat.

Whitney looked up. "Oh," he said. "I almost forgot. Jason, before you go, the gnu has something to give you for the game."

The gnu looked suddenly shy, tapping his right front hoof back and forth in the dirt.

"Only a trifle," he said. "A little poem I whipped up for the occasion—a sort of send-off, if you will."

"A poem?" Jason said. "Great. I like your poems."

"Thank you," the gnu answered. "It's actually an adaptation of Shakespeare."

"What a *sss*urpri*sss*e," the python hissed.

"Go on," said the lioness.

The gnu fetched a piece of pawed-over white paper from the back of his cage. He smoothed it out in front of him. Jason sat on a patch of grass as close to Whitney as the cage would allow. Through the bars he could feel the bear's long whiskers brush against his neck.

The gnu cleared his throat and began:

> To hit, or not to hit, that is the
>   question:
> Whether 'tis nobler at the plate to
>   suffer
> The highs and lows of outrageous
>   pitches,
> Or to take a bat against a sea of
>   fastballs,
> And by swinging, send them!
>
> 'Tis a consummation devoutly to be
>   wished!
> That tomorrow, tomorrow, tomorrow,
> Jason will rise, 'mid the sound and
>   fury
> When his coach is crying:
> "A hit! A hit! My ball game for a hit!"
> And swing a mighty blow to win the
>   game!
>
> Friends, neighbors, animals!—Take up
>   your mitts!

And look out for Jason—the king of
the hits!

When the gnu was finished the animals cheered.
The gorilla rattled the bars of his cage.

"Wonderful," the lioness said.

"*Sss*uperb!" the python agreed.

"I didn't understand every line," Whitney commented, "but it sounded like a nice piece of poetry."

"Thanks," Jason said, getting up to scratch the
gnu's chin.

"You're most welcome," the gnu replied. "It was
a pleasure."

The gorilla began jumping up and down just then,
pointing toward the gate. Mr. Handy was headed
their way, his red beard blowing in the breeze.

"Well," Whitney said. "Looks like it's lock-up
time. Good luck in the game, slugger."

"Make sure you come back and tell us all about
it on Monday," the lioness said.

"Ye*sss*," echoed the python. "We'll be *sss*izzling
with anticipation!"

"Jason star!" the gorilla bellowed.

"I'll try," Jason said. "I'll try."

He slung his bat onto the bike and after a final
goodbye rode off past the gate, down the hill to
Maple.

"You've taught him so much, Whitney," the lioness observed after Jason had gone.

"And what floorsss me," said the python, "isss that you've done it all without *ever* ssseeing a real live game!"

Whitney shrugged and tapped the newspaper still lying in front of him. "You know," he said, "there isn't much a bear can learn that isn't in the sports pages."

②

Jason's parents, Dr. and Mrs. Archibald Munson, were as proud of Jason as the animals. A year earlier, when their son first told them he was able to speak to Whitney and his friends, Dr. Munson had grinned broadly.

"Just think," he said, looking at his wife. "Our boy is the first human ever to experiment successfully with animal-human communication."

"It *is* exciting, isn't it," Mrs. Munson agreed.

She and her husband were even more thrilled when Whitney's coaching began to pay off.

"That bear sure knows his baseball," Mrs. Munson observed again the morning of the first game of the two-out-of-three championship series.

"He sure does," Jason said, finishing off a special breakfast of blueberry waffles, bacon, home fries, and apple cider.

Dr. Munson folded his napkin neatly. "Did he give you any good last-minute tips?"

10

"Well," Jason said. "He told me to concentrate on the ball. He said that even if I'm not starting, I always have to be ready."

"Sounds like good advice," his father said with a nod, as he rose to his feet. "You'd better suit up, Jason. It's almost time to go."

Jason belted up his maroon Apaches uniform and grabbed his mitt and cap.

The Munsons lived on Grove Street and Avenue C, a five-minute walk from the zoo and seven and a half minutes from the ballfield.

Though most fans hadn't begun to arrive, many of the players were stretching on the grass, warming up. The umpire was dusting off home plate. A teen-aged boy picked up a few pieces of trash that had blown into the outfield. A hot dog vendor filled his pockets with mustard packets. In right field, an old man was adjusting the lettering on the scoreboard:

	1	2	3	4	5	6	7	8	9	10	11	12	H	R	E
APACHES															
HIGHLANDERS															

OUTS 0   BALLS 0   STRIKES 0

Jason was about to run onto the field when his father squatted down next to him.

"Tell me, Jason," he said. "Now that we're actually at the ballfield, how do you feel about today's game?"

11

Dr. Munson was a psychiatrist. Jason was very used to his father asking him how he felt. He paused to think and then answered.

"I feel good about it, Dad," he said. "Though I'm disappointed that I won't be starting, I've confronted those feelings and have tried to concentrate on the thrill of being the youngest player on a team in the midst of an exciting play-off battle."

"Very good," Dr. Munson said with a satisfied nod to his wife. "That sounds very positive."

But Jason's mother wasn't so convinced by her boy's cheery response. On the walk from their apartment to the ballfield she'd noticed him looking over his shoulder toward the zoo.

"Are you sure nothing at all is bothering you?" she asked.

"Oh . . . no," Jason said.

"Really?"

"Well," Jason admitted haltingly. "Everything's fine. It's just that I wish Whitney could be here to cheer us on."

Dr. and Mrs. Munson nodded sympathetically.

"It is a pity," she said. "He's a lovely bear."

"He sure is," Dr. Munson agreed. "But unfortunately, the world at large would never believe that you and Whitney can talk."

"I know," Jason said. "But what burns me is that the zoo is so close."

His parents gazed toward the outfield. The zoo

and Whitney's cage were just behind the left field fence, beyond a shelf of rocks and a row of trees.

"Well," Jason's mother said looking at her husband. "Maybe we shouldn't be so concerned about what the public may or may not believe. Maybe I can think of some legal way to get Whitney over to see a game." Mrs. Munson was a lawyer. "But to be honest," she went on, turning to Jason, "I can't think of a single court case in which a judge has let a bear out of a zoo to see a baseball game."

Just then a boy with short clumpy hair—hair that looked like he'd cut it himself with garden shears, without the benefit of a mirror—ran up to them. It was the Apache pitcher, Bart Wagner, a fifth grader.

"Hiya," Jason said.

"Hi," Bart replied. "Hi, Dr. Munson. Hi, Mrs. Munson."

Jason's parents said hello.

"Come on," Bart said. "We've got to warm up."

"OK," Jason said.

"We'll grab some seats," Dr. Munson said. "Good luck, boys!"

The teams took batting practice while the rest of the crowd arrived. Finally, the players gathered in their respective dugouts—the Highlanders by the third base line, the Apaches by the first—for last minute pointers from their coaches.

The Apache coach, Mr. Richardson, was a sixth-grade science teacher. As usual before game time, he paced back and forth in front of the team's dugout. Jason, Bart, and the rest of the players sat quietly in a row.

"There is a great similarity," Mr. Richardson began, after a dramatic pause, "between baseball and science. Bases are aligned according to the laws of geometry. And physics describes the arc of a ball when it is hit."

Mr. Richardson paused to let his words sink in. The team stirred in their seats. Jason and Bart exchanged a glance.

"He's a good coach," Bart whispered, "but I *never* get his pep talks."

"If Aristotle and Galileo were alive today," Mr. Richardson cried, gesturing wildly, "I'm certain they'd use the baseball diamond as the basis for many of their experiments! Perhaps Isaac Newton would play shortstop, to better compute the laws of motion. Undoubtably, Copernicus would be a right fielder, to calculate . . ."

Just then a voice rang out: the umpire's.

"Play ball!"

Jason and his teammates sighed with relief. The starting nine stood up and grabbed their mitts. Mr. Richardson looked briefly surprised (somehow the umpire always cut him off before he got to the end of his pre-game speech) but then yelled, "OK, team! Pretend you're all Einsteins and go get 'em!"

3

WHITNEY, his ear pressed against the bars of the cage, did his best to follow the game. Hordes of Sunday zoo visitors passed by, but he hardly noticed them as he listened for the baseball crowd's reactions. Usually games were noisy. But this one was different.

"I say," called the gnu after a while. "Do tell. What's going on?"

"Yesss," said the python. "Thisss sssilence isss exasssperating!"

Whitney scratched his chin.

"Must be a pitchers' duel."

"Ahhh!" said the gnu. "Of course."

"A pitchers' duel?" asked the lioness.

"That's right," Whitney answered. "The crowd isn't cheering because no one's scoring any runs."

"Jason star?" the gorilla asked.

Whitney looked into the gorilla's eyes and then shook his big head.

"Sorry," he said. "Not today. It's unlikely the coach will put him in if the game's close."

"Ahh, what a pity," the gnu said. "Jason is *such* a fine chap. He deserves his chance."

Just then a giant cheer arose from the ballfield. The animals' ears stiffened. Whitney sat up on his hind legs, straining to listen.

"What is it? What *is* it?" the gnu asked.

"Tell! Tell! Tell!" the gorilla cried.

"What do you think?" the lioness asked.

"Ye*sss*, what?"

After a minute Whitney got back down on all fours.

"Well," he said. "I guess there's finally some action."

◇ WHITNEY WAS right. But the "action" was not the sort the Apaches would have hoped for. In the top of the ninth inning the Highlanders' slugger, Homer Wiggins, hit a home run, breaking a 0–0 tie.

"He hit the long ball!" yelled a police sergeant who was working the game. "He hit the long ball!"

An orthodontist who had fixed the teeth of every Highlander for the past ten years jumped in the air, cheering. The Highlander players and their coach, Mr. O'Malley, swarmed out of the dugout to meet Homer at home plate. Mrs. Wiggins, Homer's

16

mother, kissed the woman next to her, leaving a large red lipstick mark.

The Apache fans were not celebrating. The team had only one at-bat left and the Highlander pitcher, Joey Flannigan, hadn't let a runner reach third all afternoon.

Jason felt terrible for his friend Bart, who had given up the home run after pitching eight strong innings. Worse, the minute the ball disappeared over the fence, Jason knew he wouldn't play. With the Apaches behind, Mr. Richardson would never put him in.

After the Highlander cheering died down, Bart was able to pitch to the next batter.

"Come on," Jason said to himself. "Don't let up. Get this guy."

Bart recovered well. The batter popped-up and ended the inning.

"OK, OK," Mr. Richardson was saying as the Apaches jogged back to the dugout. "Let's go. This game won't be over until it's over. Come on! Hop to!"

When Bart reached the dugout, he threw down his mitt, slumped onto the bench next to Jason, and put his face in his hands.

"Don't worry about it," Jason said. "You pitched a great game."

Bart said nothing.

"All right! All right!" a hot dog vendor who was

an Apache fan cried. "We still got three more outs. We gotta nickel and dime those Highlanders to death!"

"Make it happen! Make it happen!" exhorted a piano tuner who had tuned Mr. Richardson's family piano for the past fifteen years.

"Little rally!" cried an elderly barber. He had lugged his barber chair with him to each game for the past thirty years, so he could watch the action without missing a day's business.

"You think Richardson will give Jason a chance?" Dr. Munson asked his wife.

"Oh, I hope so," she said. "Still, he is only a fourth grader. . . ."

"A fourth grader who has Whitney behind him."

"But Mr. Richardson doesn't know that. . . ."

The first two Apache batters struck out. Jason slouched on the bench with a sigh. As far as he was concerned, the game was as good as over. But the third out was to prove difficult for the Highlanders. On the next pitch, Joey Flannigan wound up and threw a curve ball that hit John Kessler, the Apache first baseman, on the elbow.

"Take your base!" the ump cried.

John trotted down to first. Judy Wheeler, the catcher, stepped up to the plate. Again, Joey wound up and threw. Judy swung and lined a solid single to center field.

With runners on first and third, the Apache fans

started chanting. But Jeremy Atwater, a good glove man, was due up. He was the weakest hitter on the team.

"There goes the game," Bart muttered.

Then Jason saw Jeremy head back toward the dugout.

"Coach is gonna pinch-hit," Bart said, excitedly.

Mr. Richardson walked down the length of the bench, looking over each player, considering whom to send to the plate. Every player he passed felt hopeful but terrified—hopeful that he or she would have a chance to be the hero, terrified he or she would strike out. Each time Mr. Richardson stopped in front of a player, Jason expected that one to be picked. But each time, Mr. Richardson shook his head and moved on down the line, closer to where he and Bart sat at the end of the bench. Now Mr. Richardson was staring at Susan O'Connell. Then, Frank Klaus. Suddenly, Mr. Richardson stood before Jason. Their eyes met.

"Get a bat," the coach said. "You're hitting for Jeremy."

Jason swallowed hard.

"All right," Bart whispered. "Win it for me."

Jason nodded and grabbed his white Louisville slugger with the blue handle. He stepped out of the dugout. The entire fourth grade cheered. Jason's teacher, Miss Martin, waved a pennant.

"Go, Jason!" she cried.

"Make it happen!" the piano tuner shouted.

The Munsons stood up.

"That's my son! That's my son!" Dr. Munson cried wildly.

"Come on, Jason! Do it for Whitney!" Mrs. Munson cheered.

As he took his warm-up swings in the on-deck circle, Jason tried to block out the noise. The coach had picked *him*. True, he'd hit well in practice lately, but there were a few older kids on the bench whom Jason had assumed would get to play before him.

"Batter up!" the umpire called.

Jason dug in beside home plate, his heart pounding. Out of the corner of his eye he saw his parents. His father was shielding his eyes against the sun. Apache and Highlander fans alike grew quiet. Jason turned toward the pitcher, trying to remember everything Whitney had told him.

Concentrate on the ball—left shoulder in—guess what he's gonna throw!

Joey Flannigan was known for his breaking pitches—his curves and sliders. Pitching from the stretch position, he held the ball in his glove close to his heart, quickly checking the runners at first and third. The catcher, Josh Zimmerman, flashed a sign. Joey nodded, wound up, reared back, and fired the ball home. Jason saw the pitch clearly. It was a little high, but it would still come over the fat part the plate. A good ball to hit. When it was nearly home, Jason committed himself. But the pitch was a slider. At the last second, the ball dipped low, away from Jason's bat.

"Strike one!" the umpire cried.

Jason stepped out of the batter's box, dazed.

"Come on, Jason!" Mr. Richardson yelled. "You can do it!"

"Good wood! Good wood!" Bart cried.

Several people in the stands were standing now.

"Why'd they put up a fourth grader?" Jason heard someone complain.

He dug in. Once again the pitcher checked the runners. Jason imagined Whitney in his cage and tried to calm himself.

"That's my son!" Jason heard his father yell from the crowd. "That's right! Him! The one with the bat!"

He'll probably throw me a curve this time, Jason thought, blocking out his dad the best he could.

The pitcher wound up and threw home. It was a curve, just as Jason had guessed; the ball curved low and away and Jason laid off it.

"Ball!" the ump cried. "One and one!"

"Good eye!" the hot dog man yelled.

"Wait for your pitch!" cried Miss Martin.

Trying to concentrate, Jason squinted toward the pitcher.

He'll come back with that slider now, he guessed.

He stepped in. The pitcher nodded to his catcher and checked the runners. Then his leg kicked and the ball came flying. It was a little high, a lot like the first one. But this time when the ball dipped down at the last second, Jason was ready for it. He brought the bat off his shoulder and swung.

The next thing he knew the ball was sailing over the third baseman's outstretched glove and the crowd was cheering. By the time Jason was standing on second base with a double, two runs had been scored and the Apaches had won.

Then his team was jumping on him. Everyone was shouting and pounding his back.

"Way to go!" Bart yelled.

Before he could catch his breath, Jason was being hoisted onto his teammates' shoulders and carried around the field. Everyone else was grabbing his sleeves. Miss Martin reached up and kissed him.

"What a hit!" his father crowed.

"Oh yes!" Mrs. Munson cried. "Whitney will be so proud!"

"Wait till I tell him it was a slider!" Jason shouted. "One of the toughest pitches of all!"

◇ BACK IN the zoo, Whitney and the other animals heard the commotion.

"What happened?" the lioness asked.

"It's hard to tell," Whitney said. "I guess somebody won."

"Who? Who?" the gnu asked.

"Can't say," the bear replied. "We'll have to wait to hear from Jason."

He reached through the bars of his cage into the trash and with his paw pulled out a newspaper.

"Well," he said to the other animals. "I'll see you all later. I've got some studying to do."

4

JASON held out a hand toward his friend. In its palm was a white hardball with red seams and a brown scuff mark.

"What's that?" Whitney asked.

"It's the ball I hit yesterday," Jason said. "I want you to have it."

The bear opened his eyes wide.

"Me?"

"Yeah," Jason said. "You."

Jason tossed the ball into the cage, where it rolled to the edge of the swimming hole. Whitney lumbered over, picked the ball up in his right paw, and held it tight, letting the feel of it seep into his skin. In all his years as a fan, he'd never actually held a ball.

"How does it feel?" the lioness asked.

"Fine," Whitney whispered. "Fine, but so small."

"Small?" Jason asked.

"That's right," Whitney said. "Small. I never

realized how difficult it must be to hit something this tiny." He studied the ball. "I can see from the scuff mark here, he threw you a slider. Nice goin'!"

Jason grinned.

"Well, don't just stand there," the gnu cried, "be a sport and throw the ball here."

Whitney looked up, surprised.

"Throw it?" he said.

"That's right!" the gnu exclaimed. "Give it the old heave-ho!"

"Go on," Jason said.

"Me?"

"Yesss! Time'sss a-wasssting!"

Whitney looked shyly at the ball sitting in his big palm.

"Well," he said with a chuckle. "Why not? If Dwight Gooden can do it, I guess I can too."

Whitney loped to the edge of his cage. He stood up on his back legs and held the ball tight against his chest. Then, in one fluid motion, he kicked out his left leg, raised his arm over his head, snapped his wrist, and let the ball fly. It shot across the courtyard and landed in the gnu's cage.

"All right!" Jason cried. "He's outta there!"

The animals cheered. Whitney began to laugh. His whiskers stretched a full six inches beyond each ear.

"Roger Clemens step aside!" he yelled. "Whitney the bear is movin' in!"

The gnu had trapped the ball with his front hooves.

"Well, don't jus*sst* *ss*stand there," the python said. "Give an a*sssp* a chance."

"Oh, dear," the gnu sighed. "Shakespeare makes no mention of how to toss a ball."

"*Ssso* what?" the snake said.

"And it is rather awkward without the benefit of paws," the gnu went on.

"Try anyway!" Jason said.

"Ah, well, here goes!"

The gnu jumped up on his back feet, gripping the ball as best he could between his front hooves. Each time, the ball squiggled away.

"I can't get ahold of the bloody thing!" he cried, exasperated.

"Goat no toes!" the gorilla gloated. "Goat no toes!"

The gnu glared at him. "I'm well aware of the fact that my feet are toeless!" he fumed.

"Relax," the lioness said. "Keep trying."

"Oh, right-o," the gnu said. "Here goes nothing."

The gnu lunged for the ball, grabbed it again between his hooves and kicked his front legs forward. The ball went flying, landed in the center of the courtyard, bounced twice, and dribbled into the python's cage.

"Not bad for a hoofed beas*sst*," the python observed. "But it'*sss* a well-known fact that a clever *sss*nake can outthrow an overly *sss*agaciou*sss* gnu."

"Let's see," Whitney said, smiling widely.

The python unwrapped himself from around his tree and, with his back end, grabbed the ball. Concentrating carefully, he steadied himself, then lashed his tail forward like a whip. The ball rocketed across the courtyard toward the lioness. When the lioness saw it screaming toward her, she panicked.

"Oh, dear, dear, dear me!" she cried, hurling herself out of its way. "Oh dear, dear, dear!"

The ball tore into the cage, ricocheted against the back wall and thundered straight into the lioness's mouth.

Thunk!

"Lion catchy!" the gorilla exclaimed, jumping up and down. "Lion catchy!"

"Got him at the plate!" Whitney cried.

"Impressive toss," the gnu conceded. "I must say asp, old boy, I didn't think you had it in you."

"If you'd pay les*ss* mind to your books*ss*," the python returned with a grin, "you'd notice the talent that lie*ss* directly before your eye*sss*."

By now, the gorilla was spinning in circles.

"Ball! Ball! Ball!" he cried. "Gorilla want ball! Give gorilla ball! Ball to gorilla!"

"Better throw it to him before he rips down his cage," Jason said.

But the ball was still implanted firmly between the lioness's jaws.

"MMMhhhmmm!" she cried. "Mmmhhmmrrmm!"

"Slap at it!" Whitney said.

"Use your tail to pry it loose!" Jason suggested.

"Bang your head againsssst the wall!" the python advised.

"Cough!" the gnu said.

The lioness, desperate, followed everyone's advice at the same time. The ball shot from her mouth and zipped across the courtyard straight to the gorilla, who caught it single-handedly.

"Ball! Ball! Ball!" he cried. "Gorilla ball!"

The lioness collapsed in the back of her cage.

"Are you all right?" Jason asked.

"I think so," she gasped. "Just a little surprised."

With the ball still held tight, the gorilla jumped up and swung from a bar at the top of his cage.

"Here you go!" Whitney called to him, raising his right front paw as a target. "Fire it in!"

"Sssmoke it!" the python dared. "Ssshow usss your ssstuff!" .

The gorilla dropped to the floor and began twirling in circles, spinning his arms above his head. He looked like a windmill during a hurricane.

"What on earth is he doing?" the gnu asked.

"He's winding up!" Jason said.

Everyone dove for cover. Just at that second, the gorilla cocked his massive right arm and let the ball fly.

"Duck!" Jason cried.

Whitney dove deep into his swimming hole just

as the ball whizzed over his head, knocked off the branch of a tree, and splashed into the water.

"Gorilla throw!" the ape cried. "Gorilla throw!"

"Wow," Whitney said, nosing the ball to the water's edge. "If we could get rid of your control problems, every major league team in the country would be after you."

Whitney heaved himself out of the swimming hole, shook off, and turned toward Jason.

"Thanks for this, pal," he said, scooping up the ball and drying it with his fur. "It'll be the center-piece of my collection. I've got just the place for it—a little ledge in the cave near my stack of base-ball cards."

Jason was astonished. Perhaps he hadn't heard right. Baseball cards?

"In your cave?" he stammered. "You have base-ball cards?"

"I sure do—and a lot more. From what I read in the papers, the Hall of Fame in Cooperstown can't compare."

"Whitney, could I see your stuff someday?"

"No one I'd rather show it to."

"Really?"

"Of course," Whitney said. "Consider yourself officially invited. But you'll have to ask Mr. Handy. There's probably some rule about visitors. If you can get his permission, though, I'd love it."

The bear yawned and rubbed his eyes.

"Listen, Jason. It's been a long day. Got to get some sleep. And I'd better stow this ball before the Hall of Fame finds out I have it and steals it away. Why there hasn't been a ball this valuable since Hank Aaron's 715th home run."

With a final smile, Whitney took the ball in his mouth and carried it toward the cave. As soon as the old bear had rounded the corner, Jason turned to the other animals, his eyes wide.

"I didn't know Whitney had baseball cards!"

"Oh yes," the gnu said. "Even more than I have Shakespeare plays—and I've twenty-one editions of *Hamlet* alone!"

Jason ran to his bike.

"Sorry to run off in such a hurry everyone, but I've got to find Mr. Handy!"

"I'M sorry, Jason," the zookeeper said a few minutes later, "I know Whitney wouldn't hurt a flea, but rules are rules. The zoo safety regulations forbid anyone except me from going into a cage."

Jason's face fell. Mr. Handy frowned unhappily.

"Well, maybe Whitney can show me his cards one at a time. . . ."

Mr. Handy shrugged. "That could take years."

Very discouraged, Jason headed home.

◊ "WHAT'S WRONG, dear?" Mrs. Munson asked as the family ate dinner. "Did something happen at school?"

"Oh no," Jason said. "School was fine. Everybody congratulated me. Miss Martin made me head of the class for the day."

"And what about the zoo?" Dr. Munson asked. "I bet Whitney was pleased."

"He was, Dad. He loved the ball."

"So?" Mrs. Munson said. "What's wrong then?"

"Well," Jason went on. "Whitney has this collection in his cave."

Mrs. Munson asked, "A collection of what?"

"Baseball cards and stuff."

"Whitney collects baseball cards?" Dr. Munson exclaimed.

"That's right," Jason said. "And tons of other stuff too. Whitney told me, and Mr. Handy said it was true."

Jason's father shook his head. "That bear never ceases to amaze me. If only my patients were half as interesting."

"That is incredible," Mrs. Munson said, "but I'm afraid I still don't see the problem."

"Well," Jason continued. "Whitney invited me to come see his stuff, but Mr. Handy says I can't because there's a rule that visitors aren't allowed in cages."

"Well, honey," his mother said quickly, "you can see the reason for that. Animals—even tame in a zoo—can turn dangerous. Not Whitney, of course, but the rules have to cover everyone. We can't expect the rule-makers to have anticipated that one day there'd be a boy who could talk to animals wanting to visit a polar bear who collects baseball cards."

"I guess not," Jason agreed. "But Mom, he invited me! He's my coach. He's not dangerous!"

"The situation is unique, I'll admit. There may

be some legal advice on the matter in one of my books. After dinner I'll look into it."

"And I'd like to have a talk with Mr. Handy," Dr. Munson said, wiping his mouth. "His unbending subservience to rules is very typical of grown-ups who are too easily intimidated by authority figures. I think I can help him with it."

While Jason and his father cleared the table, Mrs. Munson ducked into her study. A few minutes later she reappeared with a dusty old book of court cases and, as Jason and Dr. Munson looked over her shoulder, began leafing through it on the kitchen table.

"Here we are!" she exclaimed finally. "The answer to the problem. *Horace* v. *The Pittsburgh Reformatory School for Dogs.* In this case, the court ruled that a man named Horace could visit his dog in a dog reform school as long as the dog invited him. Based on this decision, we can assume that any person can visit any animal as long as they're invited."

"All right!" Jason shouted.

"Are you sure Whitney invited you, Jason?" Dr. Munson asked.

"Definitely. The others heard him. We can ask them."

"Well, *you* can ask them, son. . . ."

◇ THAT NIGHT, after Jason had gone to bed, his parents shared a cup of coffee.

"It's exciting that Whitney and Jason will get some private time alone," Mrs. Munson said.

"I couldn't agree more," Dr. Munson replied. "It should lead to the deepening of an already extremely positive relationship."

He sipped at his side of the cup and smiled.

"What a relief to know," he continued, "that while some kids are falling in with the wrong kinds of crowds, our son has such a fine role model."

6

"**W**ELL," Mr. Handy said to Jason the next day after school, "letting a boy into a cage goes against every rule I was taught in zoo-keeping school, but if your mom has found a court case and Whitney has invited you, it's fine with me."

And so it was set. Friday afternoon Whitney would sign a document and Jason would visit the cave. All week, during school and Little League practice as the Apaches prepared for game two of the championship series against the Highlanders, his mind kept wandering, imagining what the cave would be like—and what it would be like to be close to Whitney with no bars between them.

Whitney spent the whole of Friday morning inside, straightening up.

"Thisss isss an hissstoric day for zoo creaturesss!" the python said when the bear emerged.

"Whitney cleany?" the gorilla asked, dancing in circles.

"As cleany . . . I mean the cave's as clean as I can make it," Whitney replied with a stretch and a yawn. "Whew! I've got so much stuff in there."

The gorilla stopped dancing and pounded his chest, bellowing.

"What's he going on about?" the gnu asked.

"Oh, dear," the lioness said, retreating to the back of her cage. "I hope he's not getting ready to throw another ball!"

Now the gorilla was pointing, hopping on one foot.

"Foodman! Jason! Big Jasons! No-hair!" he yelled.

The other animals looked down the hill. Walking up were Mr. Handy, Jason, Dr. and Mrs. Munson, and a bald man.

"Well," Whitney said. "Looks like I'm about to get some company."

A moment later Jason and the others turned into the courtyard.

"Hi," Jason said.

The animals chorused hello.

"Guess what!" Jason said.

"What?" Whitney asked.

"I'm starting tomorrow!"

The animals cheered. Whitney smiled broadly. "Good news," he said. "Mr. Richardson finally got smart."

"What posssition?" the python asked.

"Second base!"

"You'll do well there," Whitney said. "Before you know it, Ryne Sandberg will be calling you up for advice."

Jason laughed and blushed.

"I know you've all met my parents," he said.

"Of course," the gnu said. "Always a pleasure."

Dr. and Mrs. Munson smiled and waved.

"What are they saying?" Mrs. Munson asked.

"They're saying it's great to see you."

Jason turned back to the animals and pointed to the bald man.

"And this is Mr. Maleska. He's a Notary Public. He'll be the official witness to Whitney signing the document saying I'm invited into his cave. The invitation won't count unless he signs."

Mr. Maleska smiled uneasily.

"This kid *talks* to the animals?" he whispered to Mr. Handy.

"For over a year," Mr. Handy said. "Now let's get this show on the road."

"Right-o," Mrs. Munson said.

She opened her briefcase and pulled out a long document.

"OK," she went on, handing the paper to Jason. "You read it to him."

Jason took the piece of paper and walked to the edge of Whitney's cage. The great bear stood silently on all fours. His heart was pounding, his head buzzing.

"Read it loudly, if you please," the gnu cried out. "We all want to hear."

Jason nodded, faced Whitney, and read: "I, Whitney, being a polar bear acting of my own free will, do hereby and solemnly invite my friend, Jason Munson, to visit my cave. I do this with the full understanding that Jason must leave the premises whenever I or Mr. Handy want and that each visit is subject to Mr. Handy's prior consent."

At the bottom of the page there was space for Whitney and Mr. Maleska each to sign.

"Sounds fine to me," Whitney said.

"He says it's fine," Jason translated. "He'll need a pen."

"Here ya go," Mr. Handy said.

He held a blue fountain pen through the bars. Whitney grabbed it firmly between his front paws.

"You never told me I was going to be a witness to a bear," Mr. Maleska muttered skeptically to Mrs. Munson.

"Oh, didn't I?" she asked. "I didn't think it was important. Now just sign here," she said to Whitney. She pointed.

Mr. Maleska murmured something, but drew close to Dr. and Mrs. Munson at the front of the cage. Jason slid the document through the bars. Whitney wrinkled his brow in concentration and then slowly applied the pen to the paper.

"All right," Jason said. "Good job!"

"Now notarize it, please," Mrs. Munson said to Mr. Maleska.

Cautiously, the man reached through the bars for the document and then stared at Whitney's signature. After a second, he shook his head, put on his glasses and held the paper an inch away from his face.

"Oh, dear," the lioness said. "What's going on?"

"I'm not sure," the gnu replied. "It looks like the bald chap is about to cause some trouble."

"Anything wrong?" Dr. Munson asked.

"Quite frankly, yes," Mr. Maleska said sternly.

"What?" Mrs. Munson said. "Something with the document?"

"No, no," Mr. Maleska replied. "The document itself is in order—it's the bear's signature. I can't read it!"

"It says Whitney, of course," Mr. Handy said.

"This?" Mr. Maleska responded, shoving the paper toward Mr. Handy. "It's not English! It's only a squiggly line!"

To an untrained eye, Whitney's signature did appear to be only a squiggle.

"Well, I'm sure Jason can read it," Dr. Munson said.

Jason took the document.

"This says Whitney Horatio Polarus Bearitus," Jason said.

"See?" Dr. Munson said. "Whitney's full name."

39

"I don't care what the kid says about this signature!" Mr. Maleska broke in. "For all I know it could say Mary Poppins or Genghis Khan! I can't sign!"

Jason's mother faced Mr. Maleska, her eyes as cold as ice.

"If you don't sign," she said quietly, but firmly, "I'll have to sue you for discrimination!"

Mr. Maleska's eyes opened and closed.

"Discrimination? On what grounds?"

"Discrimination against a foreigner!" Mrs. Munson said.

"Poppycock!" Mr. Maleska cried indignantly.

Mrs. Munson assumed her best lawyerly stance.

"You would sign a document if the signature was in Russian or Swahili, wouldn't you?" she asked.

"Of course."

"And you know that the law says you must sign if the person signing signs in a foreign language?"

"Absolutely."

"Then," Mrs. Munson reasoned, "you must sign when the language is Animal."

Mr. Maleska's bald spot was getting red.

"This is absurd!" he said. "Animal is not a language!"

"Just because you don't understand it, doesn't make it not a language!" Dr. Munson said.

"This is highly irregular. . . . I'm not really supposed to . . . oh well, I'll do it. But this is the last time I ever work with you Mrs. Munson!"

40

"Good," she replied. "I never realized your imagination was so limited."

Mr. Maleska took out his pen and scribbled his name. (It didn't look much different from Whitney's.) Then he took his official Notary Public seal from his pocket, opened the small bag that contained it, and pressed the device against the document.

"There," he said.

Jason breathed a sigh of relief.

The python sighed, "That wasss clossse!"

"It certainly was," the gnu agreed. "I recited the opening lines of *A Midsummer Night's Dream* to keep myself calm."

"Thank you," Mrs. Munson said as Mr. Maleska took back his pen and put away the notary seal.

"Yes, well . . ." Mr. Maleska picked up his briefcase and hurried down the hill. Whitney and Jason looked at each other and smiled.

"OK," Mr. Handy said, hefting his keys. "Prepare to be amazed."

He smiled at the white bear. Then he put a key in the lock and turned it. There was a sharp click. He pushed the door open.

"Come on," he said to Jason. "I can give you half an hour."

"We'll be waiting for you," Mrs. Munson said.

"It's so thrilling!" the lioness exclaimed.

Jason took a deep breath and walked through the cage door. His skin was tingling. Whitney stood a few steps away. Without thinking, Jason reached out and rubbed his hand through Whitney's fur. It felt thick and bristly, but softer than he'd imagined. Whitney nuzzled Jason's shoulder.

"Come on!" the bear said. "We don't have much time!"

Jason turned and waved goodbye. Then, as Mr. Handy, Dr. and Mrs. Munson, and the other animals watched, he followed Whitney past the swimming hole up a slope of rocks and into the cave.

⑦

JASON grabbed Whitney's tail and together they made their way into a dark tunnel. The air was damp and cool. After a few steps the path sloped down and veered left.

"Watch your head," Whitney said.

The top of the tunnel jutted down. Jason ducked. Then Whitney's tail tugged him to the right. Seconds later, Jason was standing next to his friend in a small room. A thin stream of light filtered through a crack in the rocks on the far wall.

"What do you think, young fella?" the bear asked.

Jason was dumbstruck. This cave was a baseball fan's paradise. He felt like an explorer who'd just stumbled onto a roomful of gold. Arranged in tall stacks and taped to the walls was the largest collection of baseball clippings imaginable. Above Jason's head was a picture of Mickey Mantle swinging a bat under a headline reading: "Mantle Hits 50th Homer." And on top of a pile to Jason's left, a yellowed, brittle piece of paper dated October 4, 1951, proclaimed: "Bobby Thomson's Ninth Inning Home Run Gives Giants Pennant over Brooklyn Dodgers." Taped to the opposite wall was the headline: "Bob Gibson and Denny McLain Square Off for the 1968 World Series."

"You like my home?" Whitney asked.

"Wow! You *do* have more stuff than the Hall of Fame!" Jason exclaimed.

Whitney laughed out loud. Jason reached over to a dusty pile.

"Your baseball cards!" he cried.

"That's right," Whitney said. "Over the years I've picked up quite a few—lots of old timers too."

Jason looked down at the cards as if he were holding a sacred artifact. His eyes widened.

"How old?" he asked after a pause.

"1953's the oldest."

"1953!"

"That's right. 1953. It's the card on top—a fellow by the name of Ed Lopat—pitched for the 1953 Yankees. Had an ERA of 2.43, I believe."

Jason stared at the faded black-and-white picture of Ed Lopat standing on the pitcher's mound, a determined look on his face.

"Wow," he whispered in awe. "Who else do you have?"

"Oh, plenty of others," Whitney replied. "Check 'em out."

Jason flipped to the middle of the deck and pulled out a card.

"Gil Hodges! From 1955. I know him. He played first base for the Brooklyn Dodgers."

Jason turned the card over and looked at the stats on the other side.

"Hey," he said. "How many homers did he hit that year?"

"Twenty-six?"

"No! Twenty-seven!"

Whitney laughed. Seen through Jason's eyes the articles and cards in his collection quadrupled in value. "Go over to the third stack from my left about halfway down," he said. "There are two pictures of Bob Feller I want you to have a look at."

Jason found the stack and sure enough, halfway down, he found two pictures of Bob Feller, the great pitcher for the Cleveland Indians. Jason shook his head. Bears are known to have long memories, but Whitney's knowledge of his collection was amazing.

"Look here," Whitney went on, laying the pictures in front of him.

Jason knelt next to the old bear.

"In this picture," Whitney said, pointing with his right paw, "Feller is about to throw a fastball. But in this one it's a curve—you can tell by the way he's snapping his wrists. Do you see?"

Jason looked at how Feller gripped the ball in each picture. "I think so," he said.

"Good," Whitney said. "Never forget that when

45

you're up at bat you can tell what kind of pitch is coming by studying the pitcher's preparation."

Jason picked up the two pictures and carefully compared them.

"You're right." Jason looked around him. "Where'd you get all this stuff anyway?"

"Here and there," Whitney said.

"But how? I thought you've been in a zoo your whole life."

"I have!"

"Then how?"

Whitney grinned and motioned Jason a little closer.

"From the trash," he whispered.

"The what?" Jason said.

"The trash," Whitney confirmed. "If you look outside my cage you'll see a garbage can. It's always been there, and every night for years I've reached down into that can, rummaged through the papers, and pulled out the sports pages. Sometimes, if I was lucky, I'd find a baseball card."

"But when did you start?" Jason asked.

"A long time ago," Whitney said, lying down on one of the few spaces of the cave floor that wasn't covered by a stack of clippings. "Let me start at the beginning. You see, when I was a cub, the old zoo-keeper, Mr. Woodbury, used to listen to baseball on the radio every day around closing time."

"Uh huh," Jason said.

"Well, one day when he was giving me my dinner, I heard a cheering sound. And then I heard an announcer say: 'He got all of it! He's going back. He's on the warning track! Oh! Goodbye! It's a home run!' "

Jason smiled. Whitney imitated the sound of a baseball announcer's voice perfectly.

"Well," Whitney continued, standing up now, "it did something to me. It was the most exciting, wonderful thing I'd ever heard! My heart was pounding! I hustled to the edge of the cage and pressed my ear up to the bars. I didn't move a muscle until the game was over and the announcers had read everyone's statistics."

"But what made you like it so much?"

"I don't really know," Whitney said. "The drama of it, I guess. Or maybe listening to that game made me feel like I was a part of something big. All I know is, that night I couldn't sleep at all! I was hooked! Starting the next day, I began listening every evening when I was fed, then each day after, counting the hours until closing time so I could hear those games!"

Suddenly, Whitney began to laugh.

"What's so funny?"

"Oh, I was just remembering something. You know, back then, I thought the ball was about the size of a grapefruit!"

"No!"

"Uh huh," Whitney said, nodding. "You see, I was imagining what size ball would fit in my paw, rather than a man's hand!"

"Wow!"

"And do you know what else?"

"What?"

"I thought the pitcher's mound was behind second base!"

"Come on!"

Whitney laughed again.

"No, no! It's true!"

"When did you realize how things really were?" Jason asked, shaking his head.

"When I started collecting the papers," Whitney replied. "Then I could see how the field really was."

"When was that?"

"Let's see," Whitney said, easing himself down on his haunches, "that's going back a long way. It must have been a few weeks after I began listening to the games on the radio. You see, after a while the thrill of only hearing the games began to fade a little. I wanted more. I wanted to see them! For a while, I must admit, I was at a loss. There was no way for me to watch television locked in this cage. But then, one day while I was pacing back and forth for the zoo visitors, I noticed a man drop his newspaper in the trash. That's when it hit me! That's how I could see the game! Through pictures! Through pictures in the paper."

48

"Did you go get the paper right away?" Jason asked.

"No, no!" Whitney said, waving his paws. "I'd've been too conspicuous. Somehow, I forced myself to wait until closing time. But as soon as it was dark and Mr. Woodbury had gone home for the night, I inched forward and reached through the bars as deep into the can as I could. I felt a lot of paper cups and bottles and other trash. But then, at the bottom, my claw brushed against it—a newspaper! I leaned over farther, grabbed it and in the twilight spread it out on the rocks."

Whitney looked at Jason.

"Reach up there and get down the top clipping," he said urgently, pointing with his paw.

Jason pulled down a yellowed article.

"Careful now!" Whitney said.

Jason held the paper flat in his palms. It was so old and crinkled he was scared it might crumble to dust in his hands. Gingerly, he laid it in front of Whitney. Whitney's eyes were blazing.

"This is the first article I ever collected!" he announced. "A Yankees/White Sox game, dated May 2, 1951. A boring game actually—the Sox won 8–3. But put yourself in my paws for a minute! It was the *first* time I had ever even seen exactly what the field looked like! For the first time I saw how spacious the outfield was. And I saw where the pitcher's mound was really located. Look at that picture there."

Whitney pointed to a picture of a man hitting a home run over the left-field fence.

"Four hundred and nine feet to center field! Three-forty-seven down the left-field line in Chicago's Comiskey Park!" Whitney exclaimed.

"OK," Jason said. "But why's that so important?"

"Because," Whitney cried, "if this player had hit the ball to center instead of pulling the ball to left, it wouldn't have gone out of the park! It would've been a fly out instead of a home run! Look at the picture closely. You can see by the way the batter is going after an inside pitch that he's *trying* to pull the ball—trying to hit that homer. It fascinated me. It was the first time I realized how much skill went into baseball! So I sat there that night long ago, under the streetlight, thinking hard about hitting. And I figured right then and there that if I was going to live in a zoo my whole life I might as well have a hobby. So here I am, all these years later, still as excited about baseball as when I first reached into that trash can."

Whitney looked at Jason and smiled.

"And it's been a good life, Jason," he said—"with these clippings to keep me company."

Whitney reached above him and pulled the ball Jason had given him a few days earlier from the ledge.

"I'll tell you," the old bear said, "out of all my souvenirs, even my oldest ones, this ball is my best."

Jason blushed. "Come on!"

Just then there was a knock on the rock outside the cave.

"Sorry guys, but it's time to lock up!" came Mr. Handy's muffled voice.

Whitney and Jason looked down the tunnel and then exchanged a glance.

"Already?" Jason said. "It seemed so quick."

"Well," Whitney said. "Time flies when you're talking baseball."

8

THE following day, during the second play-off game, Whitney and the other animals heard cheering all afternoon.

"Lots of action today, eh, Whitney?" the gnu called over.

"More than last week, anyway," the bear said, from his usual rock closest to the field.

"And how's Jason doing?" the lioness asked.

"I wish I knew," he answered with a shake of his head, "but from here it's too hard to tell."

"Foodman! Foodman!" the gorilla cried, pointing.

Mr. Handy walked quickly through the courtyard toward Whitney's cage.

"I just came from the game," he said excitedly. "Jason got a hit his first time up!"

"Smashing!" the gnu cried.

"Very nice," Whitney said wagging his head.

"A line drive to center," Mr. Handy continued.

"You should have seen the looks on his parent's faces. Dr. Munson said, 'That's my son!' and Mrs. Munson . . ."

"I wisssh we could asssk who'sss ahead," the python hissed as Mr. Handy chattered on.

"I know," the lioness agreed. "It's frustrating that we can't ask him any questions—we can understand him, but he can't understand us."

"And the umpire calls the balls and strikes with such feeling! I never knew . . ."

"What's that guy doing?" a little boy asked, pointing at Mr. Handy, who was now running from cage to cage jabbering about the game.

"Talking to the animals, dear," his mother whispered.

"But animals can't understand English."

"I know, dear. That man is deranged. Ignore him and he won't hurt you."

But Mr. Handy was hard to ignore. A crowd gathered quickly and listened. But all they heard was Mr. Handy speaking English to the animals, and Whitney and the others roaring, purring, slithering, or growling to each other.

"Hey bud," a man said finally, tapping Mr. Handy on the shoulder. "You think you're Dr. Dolittle or something?"

Mr. Handy turned and, for the first time, saw the crowd.

"Uh, no . . ." he said, haltingly. "Just trying a

new experiment in animal behavior . . . gauging their reaction to sports-related information."

He walked quickly across the courtyard. Just before he disappeared into the bird house, he turned around.

"I almost forgot! The Apaches are ahead 2–0!"

"What news!" the gnu exclaimed.

"Finally he tell*sss* u*sss*!" the python said.

"I know!" the lioness said. "I'm so glad he remembered."

"Apaches winny!" the gorilla proclaimed jumping in circles. "Apaches winny!"

"I certainly hope so," Whitney said with a laugh. "But it's only the second inning. The game's not over yet." Then to himself he murmured, "Come on, Jason!"

Whitney was right. The game wasn't over. The Highlanders came back quickly when Annie Gregory hit a three-run double in the bottom of the third. But in the fourth Shorty Rodgers stole home for the Apaches, tying the game at three.

Jason—batting seventh in the line-up—continued to have a superb game. Each time up he studied the pitcher, laid off the bad pitches, and hit the ball hard. After his second inning single, he nearly hit a home run in the fourth, flying out deep to center. By the time he banged a double down the first base line in the sixth, driving in two more runs, he was well on his way to becoming the new Apache hero.

"That kid's nicklin' and dimin' 'em," cheered the hot dog man. "He's a regular Don Mattingly—that's what he is!"

"He's making it happen!" the piano tuner exclaimed.

"That's my son!" Dr. Munson cried after Jason caught an easy pop-up. "Him! The one with the baseball mitt! That one! Right-o!"

"Wow," Mrs. Munson exclaimed in the seventh, as Jason collected his third hit of the game, another single. "Whitney must have given him some extra coaching in that cave."

"Who?" Annie Gregory's mother asked.

"Whitney," Dr. Munson said. "You know, the polar bear at the zoo."

Surrounding parents exchanged glances. Dr. Munson was known as a serious man . . . but did he say "polar bear"?

"Stop pulling our legs," one father joshed. "Really now, how'd your kid get so good in only the fourth grade?"

"I'm telling you," Dr. Munson said. "It's his coach, Whitney the bear."

Other parents laughed uneasily. Either something very strange was going on or Dr. Munson was losing his mind. Mrs. Munson took her husband's hand.

"Dear," she whispered. "Didn't we discuss this? Are you sure you should be advertising who Jason's coach is?"

"I don't see why not," Dr. Munson replied. "We're all sick of hiding it. And I think Jason should be proud of his ability to develop unusual friendships."

"Let me see if I have this straight," another father began. "You say your son is coached by a large, furry bearlike mammal that walks on four legs?"

"That's right."

"You've got to be kidding!" Mrs. Wiggins exclaimed.

"Listen," Mrs. Munson said. "Would my husband joke about something as important as our son's baseball career?"

At that, the parents knew Dr. Munson was on the level—Little League baseball was far too important a pastime to joke about. Within minutes, the news about Jason's coach began to circulate. Soon word reached the Apache dugout. By the seventh inning, Jason's teammates and Mr. Richardson had begun to look at him oddly.

"Is it really true?" Jim Lanier, a big-hitting but slow-moving sixth grader, whispered to Shorty Rodgers.

"Beats me!" Shorty said, shrugging.

Bart was especially curious. He'd often wondered why Jason spent so much time at the zoo. Until now, it hadn't occurred to him that he might be going there for a hitting clinic.

"Some nice shots today," Bart said, taking a seat next to Jason in the dugout.

"Thanks," Jason replied. "You're pitching well."

"OK, I guess," Bart said. "My curve isn't breaking right, but anyway, say—listen . . . is this stuff true? You can tell me."

"What stuff?"

"You know what stuff," Bart said. "The polar-bear stuff."

Jason looked his friend in the eyes. He'd kept his relationship with Whitney a secret because he was afraid Bart would think it was strange. But now he felt bad that he hadn't shared it. If he couldn't trust Bart who could he trust?

"Yeah," Jason said. "It's true."

Bart's eyes opened wide. "That's unbelievable!" he exclaimed.

"It's really no big deal. One day I was practicing my swing in the zoo courtyard. The next thing I knew, I heard a voice say 'Put a little more weight on your back foot. Snap your wrists more.' I looked up and there was Whitney. Since then, we've been good friends."

Bard nodded. "You know, when you put it that way it all seems pretty normal."

But other people weren't as convinced.

"It's ridiculous!" the old barber said when he heard.

"Why's that?" asked the man whose hair he was cutting.

" 'Cause baseball is a summer sport! Now, if you

told me a polar bear was coaching ice skating that'd be a different story!"

It wasn't until Homer Wiggins belted a three-run homer in the bottom of the eighth that the crowd remembered the ball game and forgot about Whitney. Suddenly the score was 7–6 Highlanders. Now, just like the week before, the Apaches had one last at bat.

"Say, who's up for the Apaches this inning?" asked the hot dog man.

"Bart Wagner," the sergeant said. "Then Karen Webster and then Jason Munson."

"All right!" the hog dog man exclaimed. "Jason'll nickel and dime 'em. Just you watch!"

Among most Apache fans, there was a feeling that, regardless of the bear rumors, Jason would deliver. In the dugout, Mr. Richardson took him aside.

"Well," he said as Bart finished his warmup swings, "it's going to be up to you. You've played a brilliant game."

Jason smiled. He welcomed the pressure. All of the other players, most of them sixth graders, nodded their agreement. In a single game, Jason had become a star. His confidence had tripled. It was hard for him to believe that one short week ago the thought of playing at all had been terrifying.

"Batter up!" the ump cried.

Bart stepped into the box. Mr. Richardson paced up and down in front of the dugout while, across the way, Whitney paced his cage, wondering what was happening in the game and how Jason was doing.

"Come on, Bart!" Mrs. Munson yelled.

"Strike him out!" the orthodontist cried.

"Good wood! Good wood!" cheered the piano tuner.

Joey Flannigan, the Highlander pitcher, looked toward home plate. The catcher signalled for a curve. Joey nodded and went into his windup. Bart concentrated on the ball.

"He's no hitter!"

"Pop one! Hit a dinger!"

Joey released the ball. But instead of curving sharply, the pitch hung over the fat part of the plate. Bart swung.

Bang! The ball took off into deep center field, over Homer Wiggins's head. Homer turned and ran after it, but before he could reach it, the ball smacked against the fence and rolled back toward the infield. By the time Homer caught up with it and threw in, Bart was on third with a triple.

The Apache fans stood up and roared.

"Bart baby!" Jason cried. "Nice shot!"

As Karen Webster dug into the batter's box, Jason grabbed his bat and stepped into the on-deck circle. He was feeling good. It should be easy to win the game now. As he took his warm-up swings he thought of how proud Whitney would be of him. . . .

"How'd you do?" Whitney would ask.

"Not bad," Jason'd answer with the easy casualness of a major league star. "I got four hits and four RBIs—all in all a pretty good day at the office."

And Whitney would smile as Jason related every detail: How in the first inning he had "gone with the pitch" and hit a fastball on the outside part of the plate to right field for a single. . . . How he had guessed every pitch the pitcher threw. . . . He'd tell Whitney about his fly ball to center field and Whitney would smile, saying, "If you had pulled it, it might have gone out."

Jason got so lost in his thoughts, he stopped taking warm-up swings. The next thing he knew the umpire was calling "batter up!" Karen Webster had popped out to the shortstop.

Jason shook himself and started toward the plate. But then he felt a tap on his shoulder. It was Mr. Richardson.

"When I touch my cap, bunt," he whispered. "We have to get that run home and tie the game up."

Jason nodded. A squeeze play, that's what the coach wanted—when the runner on third takes off as soon as the pitcher releases the ball and the batter bunts, the runner can usually score easily.

He stepped into the batter's box.

"Go, Jason!" Mrs. Munson said.

"Strike out, bear boy!" the orthodontist cried.

Jason stepped in. Bart was leading off third. Jason looked toward Mr. Richardson. Until the coach touched his cap, Jason was supposed to swing away. But Mr. Richardson's hands stayed by his sides. Joey Flannigan nodded to his catcher. Then he wound up and threw home. It was low and outside.

"Ball one!" the ump said.

"That's my son!" Jason heard his father shout. "That's him! The handsome, athletic one!"

Jason tried to block out his father and the crowd. He looked at Mr. Richardson again. His arms still hung by his side. Jason faced the pitcher. The ball came home, but on the outside part of the plate— a bad pitch to hit. Jason swung and fouled it off.

The crowd tensed. The Highlander infield shifted their positions slightly for a play at the plate. Again Jason looked back at the coach. Again no signal. The pitch was a ball. The count was 2 and 1.

"Make it happen!" the piano tuner cried.

"Concentrate!" Jason told himself.

He dug in. Joey got his sign from the catcher. Jason looked at Mr. Richardson.

He was touching his cap! That meant bunt. Jason took a deep breath. His stomach was whirling. Bart had seen the sign too, because he took a slightly larger lead off third, ready to break for home the minute Joey let go of the ball.

Joey looked at his catcher, who flashed a signal. Joey nodded. He looked to third. Bart took a step back toward the base. Joey looked home and faced Jason. He waited there for what seemed a long time.

Finally, he wound up and threw. It was a fastball heading right over the plate. Bart broke for home. Jason grabbed the bat firmly with both hands and squared to bunt. The ball came over the plate and Jason poked at it. The ball hit the bat. The crowd roared.

But instead of heading for the ground, the ball popped into the air! The catcher threw off his mask and looked over his head. As Jason ran toward first, he saw the catcher put out his mitt and catch the ball.

"Out!" the ump cried.

"Throw to third! Throw to third!" Mr. O'Malley cried from the Highlander dugout.

The catcher threw to third before Bart reached it. Double play.

"Out!" signalled the ump.

Jason felt a sharp ringing in his ears. Just like that the game was over, the series tied at a game apiece.

9

THAT night after dinner, the buzzer rang in the Munson's apartment. Mrs. Munson pressed down the intercom button.

"Yes?" she said to the doorman.

"A Mr. Richardson is here," he said.

"Mr. Richardson?" Mrs. Munson repeated, surprised.

Dr. Munson said, "I wonder what he wants?"

"He's probably come to kick me off the team," Jason sighed.

"Oh, will you stop?" his father exclaimed.

"You'd better send him up," his mother said into the intercom.

A minute later the doorbell rang.

Dr. Munson opened the door. "Hello, Mr. Richardson. Come in."

"Hello. I hope I'm not disturbing you."

"Not at all," Mrs. Munson said, running a hand through her hair.

63

Jason stood up. He steeled himself for the worst. "Hi," he said. "Guess you've come to chew me out."

The coach looked surprised.

"Chew you out?" he asked. "Don't be ridiculous! You played a great game!"

"Great game?" Jason said.

"Of course. You were brilliant!"

"But we lost," Jason complained. How could Mr. Richardson be so dumb? "I messed up the bunt."

"Forget that!" the coach said with a wave of his hand. "The squeeze play was a bad call. My fault completely! Now, I know it's awkward for me to come barging in like this, but . . . well, I've been walking for hours thinking about it and there's something I've simply got to ask you."

"What?" Mrs. Munson said.

Mr. Richardson took a big step into the room. He leaned forward and whispered into Jason's ear. "Do you really take private batting lessons with a polar bear?"

Jason stepped back.

"Uh . . ." Jason began haltingly. "Yeah, I do."

He thought Mr. Richardson was going to hug him.

"Excellent! Stupendous!" the man cried. "I was hoping it was true."

"Why?" Dr. Munson asked.

"Well," said Mr. Richardson, turning to all three of them, "We got six runs today, sure . . . but Jason and one or two others were the only kids who really

64

connected with the ball. So I was wondering if you think this bear would be willing to give the team some batting tips this week?"

Jason glanced at his parents. He figured they'd think he might have mixed feelings. And, as Jason expected, Dr. Munson knelt next to him, wrinkled his brow, and asked his favorite psychiatrist question:

"How do you feel about it, son?"

"Well, Dad," Jason replied, after a pause. "Whitney is my special friend . . . so naturally I'll be slightly jealous about sharing him with the other kids."

Dr. Munson nodded:

"But then again," Jason continued, "I wouldn't want to deprive any of them of Whitney's coaching . . . and I'm sure Whitney would enjoy it."

"Hmmm," Dr. Munson said. "It sounds as though you have a good understanding of your feelings on this issue. That's very positive."

"I can understand that you wouldn't want to share Whitney," Mrs. Munson put in, "but remember, Jason, only you can understand him—that still makes your friendship pretty special."

"A good point, Mom."

Jason turned to Mr. Richardson.

"I'll check with Mr. Handy and Whitney tomorrow. And if it's OK with them, it's OK with me."

"Wonderful!" Mr. Richardson practically

shouted. "Fabulous! Thank you! Just let me know and Tuesday's batting practice will be at the zoo."

"Fine," Jason said.

"If Whitney's able to help," his father said, "next week the game'll be over in the first inning. No need for any bunting!"

Jason frowned.

"Dad," he moaned. "Don't remind me!"

"Oh, forget about it," Dr. Munson said, laughing. "Think of the bright side. There's another game to play."

Mr. Richardson clapped Jason on the shoulder. "You'll be starting, of course, boy."

◊ "It'd be a pleasure," Whitney exclaimed on Monday. He licked his lips. "As long as Mr. Handy has said OK. But tell your coach not to expect any miracles now. I'm just one old bear. I can only work with the material I'm given. And not everyone is gonna be a natural like you."

Jason blushed.

"Maybe while you're helping them swing," he said, "you can teach me how to bunt."

"Be glad to," Whitney said. Then he shook his head. "I have to say, the way you've been swinging the bat, I'd have let you go for a hit or a sac fly at the very least."

The memory of that awful moment came rushing back. A dark look passed over Jason's face.

"Now, you stop thinking about it!" Whitney commanded, reading his friend's mind. "So you got a little over-confident. That's no big deal! Even Lou Gehrig struck out sometimes."

"Yeah," Jason said. "I know."

"All right then," Whitney said. "I'll see you tomorrow."

10

"I CAN'T believe I'm about to take batting instruction from a polar bear," Jim Lanier said late the next afternoon on the way over to Whitney's coaching session.

"I know," agreed Wendie Phillips, the third baseman and Jim's classmate. "Jason better not be kidding us."

"Don't worry," Bart said. "He's not. If Jason says the bear's for real, then he's for real."

Jim and Wendie exchanged skeptical glances.

"Maybe," Jim said. "Maybe . . ."

The team arrived just as the zoo was closing. Mr. Handy led them up the hill to the courtyard.

"Here they come!" the gnu cried. "This is a banner day in zoo history! Just think—we'll finally get to see Jason play in person!"

"I'm consssstricting with excitement," the python exclaimed.

"Tell me," the lioness said nervously. "We aren't going to have to play catch with the children, are we?"

"Don't worry," Whitney assured her. "You won't be in the line of fire. The batters'll bat next to my cage here and the pitcher'll stand halfway between me and the gnu. So the gnu, python, and the gorilla will be the outfielders."

"Gorilla catchy?" the big fellow bellowed shaking the bars of his cage. "Gorilla catchy?"

"That's right," Whitney said laughing. "Gorilla catchy."

The news pleased the gorilla no end. He began jumping and spinning in circles. And as the other animals laughed, Jason, Mr. Handy, Mr. Richardson and the team rounded the corner.

"Hi!" Jason called out.

The animals chorused hello.

"OK," Mr. Handy said. "I'll be back in an hour. Have a good workout."

"Thanks very much for the use of the bear," Mr. Richardson said.

"Think nothing of it," the zookeeper replied. "He's a fine coach."

Just then a man in a brown sweater with a camera around his neck ran up the hill.

"Sorry" Mr. Handy said. "We're closed for the day."

"Yes, but . . ." the man began. "I'm Jonathan Wilcox from the *Herald Times*. I heard a rumor you

69

were having a practice here today. Mind if I write an article about it?"

Mr. Handy looked at Jason.

"I don't know," he said. "What do you think?"

"Better ask Whitney," Jason said.

"I don't mind," Whitney said with a wave of his paw. "Just as long as he's fair and doesn't quote me out of context."

Jason passed on Whitney's answer.

"Sure," the reporter said. "I promise."

"OK, team," Mr. Richardson shouted. "Let's get going. We don't have much time!"

Bart took his position directly between Whitney and the gnu's cage. The rest of the team spread out as though the courtyard were a baseball diamond— first base between the gorilla and the lioness; second, in front of the gnu; third, near the python.

"This is our big moment, aspy old boy," the gnu breathed, bristling with anticipation.

"Yesss," the python said, unraveling himself from his tree. "I can't wait to show thessse humansss how a sssnake can tosss."

"Hit to gorilla! Hit to gorilla!" the gorilla proclaimed.

Jeremy Atwater, who was playing second base near him, took two large steps forward, away from the cage.

"Don't worry about him," Jason cried. "He's just getting into the spirit of the game."

"Sure," Jeremy said tentatively.

"OK, batter up!" Mr. Richardson cried. "Let's go! Jim—bat first!"

Jim Lanier approached Whitney's cage.

"OK," Mr. Richardson said. "Here's how it'll work. Bart will throw a few pitches. You'll take a few swings. Then Whitney'll tell Jason what you're doing wrong and Jason'll tell you."

Jim nodded and stepped up to the plate. But he couldn't resist turning around and looking at the great bear. Jim shook his head.

"What's wrong?" the coach asked.

"Wrong?" Jim said. "Nothing's wrong—except that this whole thing is dumb! Bears can't talk or coach baseball!"

Some of the other kids agreed. As much as they wanted to believe in Whitney, some of them were having trouble.

Whitney gestured to Jason.

"I think I need a little credibility. Ask Jim to ask me to do something."

Jason nodded and told Jim what Whitney had said. The other kids gathered around.

"Have him climb those rocks!" someone said.

"No! Have him act like a chicken!" said another.

"Have him stand on his head!" suggested a third.

"Don't rush me," Jim said. "I've almost got it. . . . OK, OK." Jim turned to Jason. "Tell the bear to jump in his swimming hole and do three laps of the backstroke!"

Immediately, Whitney roused himself and dove head first deep into the pool. A second later he came up.

"Wow! He's on his back!"

"He sure is!"

"That's the backstroke all right!"

Like all polar bears, Whitney was an excellent swimmer. Kicking with his hind legs and pushing with his strong forelegs, he swam back and forth three times, then heaved himself out of the water and onto the edge of the pool. He was panting hard.

"Unbelievable!" Jim Lanier exclaimed.

The reporter, who had taken pictures of Whitney swimming, shook his head in disbelief and scribbled furiously in his pad.

"Hey," Jason said. "That was great. But you're out of shape."

"No," Whitney said after he'd caught his breath. "Just old."

"No way," Jason said. "Not you." But Jason knew from Mr. Handy that Whitney was, in fact, thirty-eight years old, in polar bear years a senior citizen.

Whitney smiled and then got comfortable by the bars of the cage. Jim picked up his bat and the players took their positions.

"OK," Whitney said. "Let's see some swings."

"OK," Jason cried to Bart. "He's ready."

Bart nodded and fired a pitch. Jim, a righty,

swung and hit a pop-up to Shorty Rodgers, the shortstop.

"Another," Whitney said.

"One more!" Jason yelled.

Bart threw. This one Jim popped up to the catcher, Judy Wheeler. Whitney watched closely. His nose twitched slightly as it did when he was concentrating hard. After the second swing he raised his paw.

"I've got it," he said.

Jason motioned for Bart to hold the pitch and leaned next to Whitney's cage.

"His weight is too far forward on his left foot," Whitney began, "so he's not getting a proper, even swing. Tell him to keep his weight back on his right foot."

Jason told Jim Whitney's advice.

"Back foot, huh?" Jim said. "OK."

"Also," Whitney added, "tell him to keep his right elbow raised."

Again, Jason relayed the information. Jim nodded.

"Pitch another," Mr. Richardson yelled.

Bart fired. The ball came directly over the plate. Jim, keeping the weight on his back foot, came around on the ball and hit it hard along the ground. Shorty fielded and threw to first.

"Almost," Whitney said. "Tell him, remember to keep his right elbow raised and swing all the way through the ball."

Again, Jason relayed Whitney's words.

"Like this?" Jim asked, raising his elbow and looking over his shoulder at the bear.

Whitney nodded.

"OK," Mr. Richardson said. "Give him another."

Bart threw. This time Jim timed his swing correctly. He swung and connected perfectly. The ball shot straight ahead.

"Nice hit!" Mr. Richardson said.

"It's mine!" the gnu cried. "Mine I tell you! Oh yes! Oh happy day!"

Though they couldn't understand what the gnu was saying, the kids turned and watched in amazement. The gnu stood on his back legs, jumped in the air and caught the ball spectacularly between his two front hooves. The reporter snapped a picture.

"Nice catch!" Jason yelled.

"A trifle," the gnu replied. "See aspy, old boy, there's more to me than just good looks and a good mind."

"If you can make yoursssself believe that, more power to you," the python replied.

The gnu ignored the python, dropped the ball, and kicked it back into the courtyard.

"Let's see another hitter!"

So the practice continued.

"Jason, tell him to keep his knees bent!" Whitney cried about one batter. "He's taking his eyes off the ball! Tell him to concentrate!"

Jason did.

"Tell her to get closer to the plate," Whitney said about another. "How can she hope to hit a pitch on the outside corner standing so far away?"

Whitney tailored his advice to fit each player. If a batter had an unusual swing, he didn't try to change his style, but, rather, showed the batter how to do better what he was doing naturally.

In the outfield, the gnu, python, and gorilla each saw plenty of action. The python made easily the most impressive play of the day when Wyatt Torple hit a hard line drive into his cage. In a fluid motion, the python wound up his tail end, snagged the ball and whipped it home, catching a runner who was trying to score from third. And though the gorilla could never quite catch a ball, he demonstrated repeatedly that he had the best arm in the city. After each fumble, he would chase the ball and jump up and down in a mad frenzy, yelling, "Gorilla catchy!" Then he would reel around several times and throw it into the courtyard with all his might. The first throw dented the metal trash can next to Whitney's cage. Another cracked the rim of a drinking fountain. It didn't take long for the kids to learn about running for cover whenever the gorilla began his unique windup.

Whitney had just seen the last batter when Mr. Richardson declared the practice over. As they left, the players ran to Whitney's cage to thank him.

"Thanks, Mr. Bear."

"I think I can hit to the opposite field now."

"I've learned not to go after the high fastball!"

"You've helped a lot," Mr. Richardson said.

Whitney nodded to them all. Then the reporter came by, positively beaming. This was the story of his career.

"I'll be sure to send you a copy of my article," he said as he followed the others toward the gate. "Thanks!"

"Everyone loved you!" Jason said. "Did you have fun?"

"Oh, yes," Whitney sighed happily. "Some good hitters out there. But what about you? Aren't we gonna work on your bunting?"

"Well . . . sure. I thought there wasn't time."

"There's always time for you, pal. Mr. Handy won't mind. Pick up a bat."

"But who's going to pitch? Should I run and get Bart?"

"Nah," Whitney said. "Don't bother. Let's give the gorilla a chance."

The gorilla started twirling around in his cage.

"Gorilla pitch! Gorilla pitch!"

"He'll kill me!" Jason exclaimed.

"No, he won't," Whitney laughed. "He can throw slower if he tries. Hey," he yelled across the courtyard, "just ease the ball over the plate. Go on," he continued to Jason. "Toss him the ball."

Jason obeyed.

"No fassstballsss!" the python warned.

"Easy does it!" the gnu said.

"Gorilla throw soft!" the ape assured them.

Nervously, Jason stepped up to the plate.

Doing his best to concentrate, the gorilla wound up.

"Be careful!" the lioness exclaimed.

He spun around twice and let the ball go as gently as he could. Even so, it shot forward faster than any Little League pitcher could possibly throw.

Jason squared off and bunted. But as in the game, the ball popped up. Disgusted, Jason kicked the side of Whitney's cage.

"Relax," Whitney said. "I see your problem. You're lunging at the ball. Here's what you do. When the ball is coming, turn and face the pitcher. Don't stand sideways. Crouch down and keep your eyes nearly level with the bat. Space your hands wide apart. Let the ball hit the bat. Don't slap at it."

Jason nodded and threw the ball back to the gorilla.

"Try to make the next one even slower." Whitney cried.

"Gorilla throw underhand!"

He did just that. Still, the ball sped over the plate as powerfully as Bart's best fastball. Jason turned, crouched, and let it hit the bat. The ball skittered along the pavement.

"Better," Whitney said. "But don't lean toward

first base. Remember, in most cases a bunt is a sacrifice. Don't think about getting a hit. Just get the ball on the ground."

Mr. Handy walked into the courtyard and stood quietly by the python.

"Hi," Jason said. "Whitney's helping me with my bunting."

"Take your time," Mr. Handy said.

"Now, don't punch at the ball so much," Whitney told Jason. "And try to keep your hands a little farther apart."

Once again, Jason threw the ball back to the gorilla and the big ape pitched.

Mr. Handy and the animals watched the workout until it was nearly too dark to see.

By the time Jason made it home for dinner, his coach was snoozing in his cave, one tired, but happy, bear. He dreamed not of the Yankees or the Red Sox, but of the Highlanders and the Apaches—and the biggest game of all coming up.

11

THE next day when Jason showed up for breakfast, his parents were sitting at the dining-room table with the morning paper spread before them.

"Hey," Mrs. Munson cried. "You're a star!"

"What?"

"Come see!"

There, on the front page of the B Section, was a picture of Jason holding a bat, with Whitney standing by the edge of his cage. The headline read: "Polar Bear and Boy Help Little League Team."

"Sit, sit," his father said. "I'll read it to you!"

As Jason sat, his father began:

"You may have heard of a performing seal or a dancing elephant, but have you ever heard of a polar bear that coaches baseball? Well, one lives right here in town

79

at the City Zoo. His name is Whitney and yesterday the Little League Apaches held batting practice outside his cage.

'Whitney's a baseball genius,' said Jason Munson, the bear's closest friend and star Apache player. 'He's spent his life studying the greats like Ted Williams, Hank Aaron, and Bob Feller so he knows pretty much everything about hitting, pitching, and fielding.'

During the practice, Whitney's experience showed. In only an hour he had the Apache batters swinging the bat as they never had before. Tom Richardson, the Apache's coach, didn't hide his pleasure. 'That bear is going to help us win the championship,' he stated confidently.

'He straightened out my swing,' said Apache right fielder Jim Lanier.

'He told me to be more patient at the plate,' commented shortstop Shorty Rodgers.

Whitney gave his tips to Jason who then passed them on to the rest of the team. If you think this sounds incredible, hold onto your mitts—there's more! In this practice, the outfielders were a python, a gnu, and a gorilla. And it is the assessment of this reporter that the gorilla's arm has major league potential.

'All the animals love the game,' young Munson said. 'But Whitney is a special fan. He should help us beat the Highlanders.'

The big game is this Saturday at 1:30. But come early—seats will be going fast!"

Dr. Munson stopped reading.

"My son—in the paper!" he said.

"It's so exciting!" Mrs. Munson exclaimed. "You deserve a celebrity breakfast."

◇ THE ENTIRE fourth grade was excited too. The minute Jason entered his classroom he was surrounded.

"Can you get me his autograph . . . I mean his pawprint?"

"During basketball season, could he help me with my jump shot?"

Even Miss Martin couldn't contain herself. Before a spelling test she drew Jason aside.

"If you get any offers from talk shows, I'd be glad to appear with you."

It wasn't until lunchtime that he encountered some of the older and more skeptical students.

"There's Mr. Polar Bear!" a sixth grader yelled as Jason stood on the foodline with his tray.

"Hey," another said to a kitchen worker, "give him a plate of seal meat!"

"Lay off him!" a voice cried.

Jason looked up. It was Jim Lanier.

"Why?" the first boy asked.

"Because the bear is for real. I saw it. In fact, he helped me so much I'm going to hit a home run Saturday."

"Aw come on . . . don't you see that Munson is making a fool outta you?"

"That's what I thought at first," Jim said. "Now beat it!"

The other boys shuffled away.

"Ignore them," Jim said to Jason. "They're jealous. The only animals they can play with are stuffed."

Jason nodded.

"Hey," Jim continued, "why don't you come sit over here with me?"

Jason couldn't believe his ears.

"I'd love to," he said, "But I have to stay with my class."

"Oh, right," Jim said. "See you at practice then."

"Wow!" a classmate exclaimed, as Jim walked away. "Jim Lanier asked you to sit with him!"

"Forget about it," Jason said. "It's no big deal."

It was a big deal. Jason's class fussed over him all day. But the more they did, the less Jason enjoyed it. Something about all the attention bothered him. That afternoon, for the first time in weeks, he didn't hit well in practice.

"You OK?" Bart asked after Jason had taken his swings. "You seem kind of down for the school hero."

Jason smiled weakly.

"I guess I'm just thinking," he said.

"What about?"

"About Whitney."

"He's a great bear," Bart said. "What's bugging you about him?"

"Nothing about him," Jason said. "But, well . . .

let's face it, today I'm a hero, but I'd be nothing around this school if it wasn't for his help."

Bart shook his head.

"Not necessarily true," he said, "I'll admit Whitney helped, but you're the one with the talent."

"I guess," Jason said. "Still, he's done a lot for me and I haven't done a thing for him."

"He doesn't expect anything," Bart said.

"I know," Jason said. "But I still want to give him something special."

"Like a gift?"

"Exactly," Jason said. "But he already has one of the best baseball-card collections in the country. What else could he possibly want?"

"How about some special food?" Bart suggested. "Maybe he'd like to try ice cream."

"Maybe," Jason replied, "but I doubt Mr. Handy'd allow it. Those animals have a pretty strict diet."

Just then Mr. Richardson called for Bart to practice his pickoff move to first.

"Gotta go," Bart said.

Jason kept thinking for the rest of the practice. But it wasn't until he was biking home that his mind cleared. In a flash, he knew just what to do for Whitney. . . .

◊ AT HOME, Jason pulled one of his mother's law books off the shelf, flipped to the subject index and moved his finger down the page.

"Let's see," he said to himself. "Bear . . . bear."

There was a case pertaining to beans and another to beaks, but none to bears. Undeterred, Jason checked under "polar bears." Again, nothing. He was just about to look under "arctic mammals" when his mother walked into the room.

"Dear?"

Jason turned.

"Hi, Mom."

"What are you doing?"

"Just looking something up in your books."

"What?"

"I wanted to see if there was a case that could legally help us get Whitney out of the zoo and to the third game."

Mrs. Munson thought.

"Hmmm, that's awfully nice of you to think of, but I'm not sure . . ."

"He's such a good old bear," Jason went on, "and he's done so much for me, I've just . . ."

"What did you say?" his mother interrupted.

"I said he's such a good old bear."

Mrs. Munson's eyes began to sparkle.

"What Mom? Did you get another idea?"

"Something just occurred to me," she said excitedly.

"What?" Jason asked.

"Well," Mrs. Munson said. "I must admit that Whitney being elderly changes things a bit."

"Changes what things?"

"It's in a case I read in law school. If only I can remember where it was. . . . Let's see now!"

Mrs. Munson sat at her desk and turned on her law computer.

"It involved a cat," she said.

"A cat?"

"And it was in New York before 1930."

"So?"

"So, be patient. I think it might relate to your problem."

Mrs. Munson typed, "Cat, New York, date before 1930" into the computer and pressed a button. Jason watched as the machine did its work. Soon the screen lit up. It read: "There is one case."

"That's it!" Mrs. Munson cried.

She pressed another button. On the screen flashed the summary of *Haddox* v. *The State of New York*. Mrs. Munson read it aloud.

"In 1924, in New York, Millard Haddox sued the state for not letting him take his elderly pet cat to the race track. The judge ruled that an elderly animal has the inalienable right to attend sporting events as a reward for living a good life, so long as that animal sincerely loves the sport in question and isn't dangerous."

"All right!" Jason cheered. "So Whitney can go to the game?"

"Well," Mrs. Munson said. "Maybe. First, we'll have to go to court and prove three things."

"What?" Jason asked.

"First," Mrs. Munson continued, "that Whitney's old, second that the one thing he'd like to do above all else is go to a ball game, and third, that he isn't dangerous."

"That shouldn't be too much of a problem," Jason said.

"Probably not," his mother agreed. "But we'll have to get Mr. Handy, and maybe Mr. Richardson to testify—along with you, of course."

"They'll do it for Whitney."

"I'm sure they will," Mrs. Munson replied. "But Jason, don't expect any miracles. Remember, most people feel polar bears should be in the Arctic or kept in cages!"

(12)

JASON wore a sports coat and tie for his day in city court.

"Here's how it'll work," his mother said to Jason, Mr. Richardson, and Mr. Handy. "This is a hearing. You'll go up on the stand one by one and the judge will ask you questions. Just relax, listen, and be truthful, OK?"

Everyone nodded, and together they walked across the large marble lobby of the court building and through a door marked "Courtroom C." At the front of the chamber was an elevated desk, and below that the witness stand. The rest of the room was lined with benches. Mrs. Munson directed them all into the front row just as a serious-looking man in a suit entered through a side door.

"Who's that?" Jason asked his mother.

"The court clerk," she said.

"City Court now in session!" the man announced. "The Honorable Judge Warriner presiding!"

"Stand up!" Mrs. Munson whispered.

Everyone stood. The side door opened again and Judge Warriner, an old man with gray hair, dashed into the room, his long black robe billowing majestically behind him. He sat at the elevated desk.

"Please be seated," he said.

Everyone sat. As the judge put on a pair of spectacles and shuffled through some papers, the clerk spoke again.

"This hearing is in session," he stated. "Judge Warriner will be considering several issues in regard to Whitney the polar bear, resident of the city zoo. Firstly: if said bear is elderly. Secondly: if said elderly bear's one and only desire is to attend a baseball game. And thirdly: if it is said elderly bear's one and only desire to attend the previously mentioned baseball game, whether said bear may cause undue agitation, alarm, or harm to spectators thereat."

The clerk sat down. Jason and his mother exchanged a glance.

"Don't worry," she whispered to him. "That's just court talk."

Jason nodded.

"I know. Like on TV."

The judge looked up from his notes.

"I'll hear from Mr. Thomas Richardson first," he said.

The coach nodded and walked to the stand. The clerk asked him to raise his right hand.

"Do you swear that your testimony will contain nary a falsehood?"

"I do," Mr. Richardson said.

"Please be seated."

Judge Warriner gazed down from his desk. "You are the coach of the Apaches?"

"Yes, sir," Mr. Richardson replied.

"Tell the court how this bear has helped your team."

Mr. Richardson leaned forward and eagerly told the judge:

"He helped Jim Lanier hit line drives. He taught Shorty Rodgers how to hit to the opposite field. He showed Wendie Phillips how to hit a pitch on the outside corner. I tell you, Judge, I wouldn't have believed it if I hadn't seen it with my own eyes. But I'd say that bear knows more about baseball than Whitey Herzog!"

A longtime baseball fan, Judge Warriner responded to this final piece of information with an impressed upward turn of both eyebrows. Like most fans, the judge considered Whitey Herzog, the manager of the St. Louis Cardinals, one of the smartest men in baseball.

"Your testimony has been most illuminating," he

said. "You have made Whitney's baseball genius evident to the court. You may step down. Next witness!"

"That's you," Mrs. Munson said to Mr. Handy, who immediately stood up. For this important appearance, Mr. Handy had combed his long red beard and wore a freshly pressed green flannel shirt.

"Do you swear that your testimony will contain nary a fib?" the clerk asked.

"Of course," Mr. Handy answered.

"Now, tell me, sir," the judge began as Mr. Handy took his seat. "As Whitney's keeper, how would you describe his age?"

"About as old as a grandfather," Mr. Handy said.

Judge Warriner nodded.

"How long have you been employed at the zoo?" he asked.

"Ten years, Your Honor."

"In those ten years has Whitney ever harmed or intended to frighten anyone in any way?"

"Never," Mr. Handy replied, looking intently at the judge. "That bear's as harmless as a puppy. Why, once a sick bluejay fell out of his tree into Whitney's cage and that kind old bear picked him up in his mouth and held him there till he could get my attention."

The judge nodded vigorously. "Impressive."

Speaking with more confidence now, Mr. Handy continued:

"He's one of the most popular animals we have in the zoo. Among his peers as well as the public."

The judge looked the zookeeper in the eye.

"Is it your opinion that this bear would like to see a baseball game above anything else?"

"Absolutely," Mr. Handy said.

"Very good," the judge declared. "And most enlightening. You have shown Whitney to be an elderly mammal of great popularity and integrity. You may step down. Next witness!"

Mrs. Munson squeezed Jason's hand.

"You're up," she said.

Jason swallowed and resolutely approached the stand.

"Do you swear that your testimony will contain nary an assorted prevarication?" the clerk asked.

"What?" said Jason.

"Do you promise you won't lie?" the clerk asked.

"I do," Jason replied.

Jason took his seat on the witness stand. The seat was wood and felt hard.

"Now, son," Judge Warriner said warmly. "There are a few things I'm curious about. First, tell us about your friend Whitney. When did you first meet? And, um . . . when did you have your first chat?"

Jason cleared his throat and told his story.

". . . and the next thing I knew Whitney was giving me a batting lesson. Then we started talking about the 1955 World Series."

The judge removed his spectacles.

"The Brooklyn Dodgers won that one," he said.

"Right!" Jason said.

"I'm a Brooklyn fan from way back," the judge said, smiling. "Boy, was it ever good to see them finally stick it to those Yankees."

"It certainly must have been satisfying, sir," Jason agreed.

"Johnny Podres pitched a two-to-nothing shut-out in game seven!" the judge exclaimed. "But enough of that. Do go on."

"Yes sir," Jason said. "It was Whitney who first told me all about that series. After that we became great friends. And then I became friends with the gnu, python, gorilla, and lioness."

"And have these animals followed your baseball team as well?"

"Yes sir," Jason said.

The judge nodded vigorously.

"That's all I need to ask, Jason—unless you have anything you'd like to add."

"No, that's it, sir," Jason said. "Only it would mean so much for Whitney to see our game. He's everybody's coach. Just like Mr. Richardson."

Judge Warriner nodded a final time.

"Thank you, son," he said. "You may step down."

Mrs. Munson grinned proudly at Jason. He and Mr. Handy exchanged a smile. Then, they all looked up at the judge's desk.

"Well," Judge Warriner began, after replacing his glasses and shuffling once more the papers before him. "Everything seems to be in order. Mrs. Munson, as usual, you've done a splendid job. It seems clear that Whitney is a kindhearted elderly creature, not dangerous in any way. He loves baseball and he loves Jason. Therefore, based on the precedent of *Haddox* v. *The State of New York*, it seems fitting that the bear be allowed to go to Jason's game as a reward for a long life well lived."

"Yippee!" Jason cried.

"But! There is one thing. . . . I do think it's wrong to deprive the other animals who are the boy's friends of also seeing the game."

Mrs. Munson's eyes opened wide.

"Well, Your Honor," she stammered. "I hadn't considered . . . I mean they aren't baseball fans like Whitney and *Haddox* v. *The State of New York* clearly states that the animal must be . . ."

"All five animals will go!" Judge Warriner exclaimed, pounding his desk with his gavel. "I've decided!"

"But is that legal?" Mrs. Munson asked.

"It is now!" the judge said. "That is, if it's OK with Mr. Handy."

"Sure it is," the zookeeper said.

"All right!" Jason cheered.

Still congratulating each other, the group headed toward the door.

"One last thing before you go!" the judge called. Everyone stopped.

"Yes, Your Honor?" Mrs. Munson said.

The judge smiled broadly. "Just make sure you save me a seat!"

13

"**T**HIS place is gonna be jam-packed, I'm telling ya," the hot dog man told the sergeant the morning of the deciding game. "Jam-packed."

The policeman nodded. "That article on the bear is all anyone's talkin' about."

"You're tellin' me," the hot dog man said. "And ya know what I heard?"

"What?"

"I heard that the animals themselves are gonna be here!"

"No!"

"Yes!"

Indeed, word of Whitney and the others had spread through the city like oil on a baseball glove.

All the regulars—the orthodontist, the piano tuner, the barber, students, parents, and teachers— arrived by ten-thirty to claim their usual spots. By eleven, people were pouring into the park, filling the bleachers. And at eleven-thirty the press arrived. By game time, there were so many newspeople it was necessary to create a separate area for them behind a police barricade.

At noon, the Parks Commissioner ordered that three hundred folding chairs be set up to accommodate the growing crowd. At twelve-thirty, a troop of mounted police trotted in from center field. Just behind them came Jason's parents who had been at the zoo helping Mr. Handy and their son get the animals ready.

From across the field, they heard a shout: "There they are! There they are!" Dr. and Mrs. Munson looked up. Charging toward them, waving microphones and lugging cameras, were the reporters. Before they knew it, the two of them were surrounded. One reporter took the lead and started firing questions.

"You say that you're the proud parents of Jason?"

"That's right," Dr. Munson replied.

"How long has your son been coached by the bear?" cried a woman with a notepad.

"Oh, about a year," Mrs. Munson said.

"Tell me," asked a third reporter, "does your son actually talk to the animal, or does he just pretend?"

"He really talks, of course," Mrs. Munson said.

A murmur and some laughs rippled through the crowd.

"Forgive me, sir and ma'am," the first reporter said, "but you must admit that's rather hard to believe. How do you explain it?"

Dr. Munson looked thoughtful for a minute.

"Well," he said, "it's a fact that there are many aspects of the human mind that have yet to be researched thoroughly. Man's animal communicatory ability is one of them. I think it may not be so extraordinary that Jason and Whitney talk."

"Come now. Isn't your son living in a kind of fantasy world?"

Dr. Munson blinked. His cheeks turned red.

"Fantasy world?" he said. "Because you cannot comprehend it doesn't make it fantastic. You obviously lack the depth to appreciate the expansiveness of my son's mind!"

The crowd hushed, impressed, just as Judge Warriner fought his way toward the bleachers. He was dressed in shorts, sneakers, and a baseball shirt. On his head was a Brooklyn Dodgers cap. In his right hand, a mitt.

Immediately, a reporter called out.

"Judge! Judge! Do you believe this talking bear story?"

Judge Warriner faced the woman. Ten microphones were instantly shoved at his face.

"Why not?" the judge declared. "I've been deciding cases for thirty-nine years and believe me, I've seen much stranger things than that! Why once

I saw a girl sue her parents for making her go to bed before the eleven o'clock news, and only last week I . . ."

"Hold it," Mrs. Munson broke in. "Here come the animals now!"

She pointed to deep center field.

Moving slowly toward home plate were Mr. Handy, Jason, Whitney, the gnu, the lioness, the python, and, looming above them all, the gorilla.

"It's true!" Annie Gregory's father cried. "There they are!"

"Keep back!" the sergeant directed. "Give them room! Give them room!"

The crowd was on its feet.

"What do you think?" Jason asked Whitney as his friend took his first steps ever on outfield grass. "Is it like you imagined?"

"It's better," the old bear said with a grin.

"I say," the gnu cried, prancing toward second base. "All this grass is inspiring!"

"Yesss," the python agreed. "I finally have ssspace to ssstretch."

"And look at all the people!" the lioness added.

"Gorilla big room! Gorilla big room!" the gorilla announced, pounding his chest.

As soon as Jason and the others reached the infield, the Apaches ran from the dugout to greet them. The reporters took this as a cue and gathered around as well.

"Hey!" Wyatt Torple cried to Whitney. "I've been practicing what you told me all week!"

The reporters busily clicked pictures and scribbled notes.

Whitney lowered his head, both embarrassed and pleased by all the attention.

"Hello again everyone!" Mrs. Munson said, leading Judge Warriner through the crowd.

"This is the man who arranged for you to come here today," Jason told the animals.

Jason translated their thanks; the judge was enchanted. Just then, the umpire joined the gathering.

"Excuse me," he said. "I hate to break up the party but we have a championship game to play. Let's get these animals to their seats."

"Right," Mr. Richardson said. "Back to the dugout, team."

Jason tugged on the umpire's arm.

"There is one thing, sir," he said.

"Yes, son?"

"Well, the gorilla wanted to know if he could throw out the first ball?"

"What?" the ump said.

The reporters drew closer, listening intently.

"The gorilla?" The umpire looked confused. In all his years of officiating he'd never heard of that one!

"Can he throw?" he asked, glancing quizzically at second base where the gorilla waited for a sign from Jason.

"Can he throw?" Mr. Handy said. "Just you wait!"

The ump consulted his watch and shrugged. "Well," he said. "We've still got eight minutes until game time. I don't see why not."

"Thank you," Jason said, giving the gorilla a thumb up and tossing him a ball.

"Go ahead," he said.

For a few seconds, the gorilla simply stared at the ball in his paw, unbelieving. Then, in a manic burst, he began jumping up and down in the air, whooping with delight.

"Gorilla throw! Gorilla throw!"

Then he did a backwards somersault, landed on his feet, and broke into a flat-out run toward center field.

"The gorilla's loose!" a woman cried.

"Help! Protect the children!" shouted another.

A mounted policeman took off after the ape.

"There's nothing to be alarmed about!" Mr. Handy yelled. "He's going to throw out the opening ball!"

This news relaxed the crowd. The mounted policeman turned back.

"I say," the gnu said to Jason, "mind if I have a go at catching it?"

"Why not?" Jason answered, holding out his glove.

The gnu took it in his mouth and trotted over to home plate. By now, the gorilla was twirling in circles in deep center field.

"What's he doing?" someone yelled.

"He's having a seizure!"

"No! No! He's getting ready to throw! Look out!"

That fan was right. The gorilla was into one of his windmill windups. Holding the ball in his right paw, he spun in tight circles as fast as he could while simultaneously whipping his arms around his head. (Spinning so fast in so many different directions, it was a near miracle he didn't take off.) Then, with a powerful thrust, he let the ball go.

Up, up, up into the sky it soared. The crowd was awed.

"Dave Winfield look out!" the hot dog man yelled.

"It's a UFO!" chimed someone else.

Few people noticed who was waiting for the ball at home plate, until a little boy shouted, "Look!"

"It's the gnu!" cried his mother.

"Now I've seen everything!" his dad exclaimed.

The gnu stood calmly by home plate on his back legs now, mitt on his front left hoof, waiting for the ball overhead.

"I say," the gnu worried. "I wonder if it'll ever descend?"

But descend it did. After what seemed an eternity, the ball arced over the infield and dropped out of the sky smack into the gnu's glove.

The crowd cheered.

"Fine toss," Whitney commented to the other animals. "Willie Mays would have been proud of that throw."

In center field, the gorilla pounded his chest in pleasure.

"Gorilla throw!" he cried. "Gorilla throw!"

The gnu pranced out to second base.

"Sssplendid catch!" the python said. "Ssshake-ssspeare would have written a play about it."

"Not a play," the gnu said modestly. "A sonnet, perhaps, but I think not a play."

Just then, the gorilla finished a back flip, skipped to right field, did ten cartwheels around the infield, and finally landed next to the gnu and took a deep bow.

Even Mrs. Wiggins allowed herself a small smile.

"My son is close personal friends with that go-rilla!" Dr. Munson informed everyone near him.

"What an athlete that ape is!" the judge ex-claimed. "He could get Olympic medals in the long jump, the javelin, gymnastics, and the hundred-meter dash!"

It took a full five minutes for the crowd to calm down. All the while the umpire cast periodic glances at his watch. At last, he grabbed a megaphone from one of the policemen.

"OK," he cried. "Let's play ball!"

"SORRY, team," Mr. Richardson said as they took their seats in the dugout. "I have some bad news—today I'm going to forgo my customary pep talk."

The players exchanged glances. This was hardly bad news.

"Now, I know it's upsetting," Mr. Richardson continued, raising his hands as if to stop a wave of protest. "I had some remarks prepared comparing baseball to the creation of the solar system, but that speech will have to wait, because Jason tells me that the gnu has asked to say a few words instead."

The gnu? A pep talk by a gnu?

The players smiled. Mr. Richardson nodded to the animal, who trotted to the front of the dugout. Jason got up and stood by his side.

"Thanks for agreeing to translate for me," the gnu said.

103

"No problem," Jason replied.

"And please remember," the gnu went on, whispering, "that for this little talk to have the appropriately stirring effect, it's important that you render your translation with a little drama."

"I'll do my best," Jason said.

"Very well, then," the gnu replied. "Let's start, shall we?"

He turned to the players, rose to his hind legs, and cleared his throat. A mild breeze blew back his short mane.

"Hello chaps," he began. "I do hope you'll win today. To assist you in that pursuit I've reworked a speech that Abraham Lincoln, your country's great sixteenth president, gave at Gettysburg."

Jason echoed the gnu's introduction; the players and Mr. Richardson nodded their heads. Whitney and the other animals moved close. The gorilla sat on the dugout steps.

"Goat speech!" he said.

"Yes, dear," the lioness replied, lying down next to him. "Isn't it exciting?"

The gnu took a deep breath, wrinkled his brow, and threw himself passionately into his address:

"Four score and seven years ago, Abner Doubleday brought forth on this continent the game of baseball, conceived for sport and dedicated to the proposition that the best team must win!"

The gnu paused, letting the full weight of his

words sink in. Jason puffed out his chest and translated as dramatically as he could.

"Now," the gnu continued, "we are engaged in a final ballgame, testing whether our team can long endure!"

Jason translated. The gnu thrust his right hoof forward and gave the Apaches a hard stare.

"The world will little note nor long remember what I say here!" he exclaimed.

Again, Jason translated, pointing forcefully with his right hand.

"But it will never forget how you play here! It is for you, the players, to demonstrate that the first two play-off games shall not have been played in vain! That the team of Apaches in a game played by Apaches and for Apaches, shall not perish from this earth!"

The gnu finished with a great craning of his neck, then collapsed to all fours. As Jason uttered the final words of the speech, he threw himself down on one knee, holding his hands to his heart. When he was done, something surprising happened—everyone in the stands, Apache and Highlander fans alike, stood up and cheered.

"What?" Mr. Richardson said.

A sneaky reporter had stuck his microphone into the Apache dugout; the entire speech had been broadcast to the crowd, among whom there were very few dry eyes.

"That gnu could have quite a career in politics!" Judge Warriner commented.

"Are we ready?" complained the umpire. "Or perhaps the lion wants to juggle? Or maybe the snake wants to try the rhumba?"

Mr. Richardson shook his head.

"All right!" the ump cried. "Batter up!"

15

THE Highlanders took the field. Calm as ever, Joey Flannigan stood on the mound. Homer Wiggins waited patiently in center field. Annie Gregory leaned forward on her toes, at the ready at shortstop. Shorty Rodgers scrambled for his bat, took a few warmup swings, and jogged up to the plate.

"OK, Shorty!" Mr. Richardson called. "Get us started!"

Joey took the sign from his catcher and threw. The ball zipped hard across the outside part of the plate.

"Strike!" the ump cried.

The Highlander fans roared. Whitney glanced at Jason.

"That boy throws hard," he said.

Jason nodded and looked back at the field. Shorty was rubbing dirt on his hands. Coolly, Joey waited for his catcher's signal. Shorty stepped back up to the plate. The catcher made a target with his mitt. Joey nodded, wound up and threw. It was a curve and a good one. Shorty lunged at the ball, which dribbled weakly off his bat down the third base line. But even though it was a terrible hit, Shorty had a good chance of making it to first. He was fast and the third baseman, Eric Hadden, had to retrieve the ball in a hurry to make a play.

"Don't throw!" Joey yelled. "You'll never get him!"

But Eric whipped the ball to first anyway . . . right over the first baseman, Nina Spine's, head. While she scrambled after it, Shorty jogged to second. The Apache fans cheered and whistled.

"All right!" the hot dog man cried. "What did I tell ya! That's what nickel and dimin' is all about! Forcing those mistakes!"

The animals were equally thrilled.

"Ripping good!" the gnu proclaimed.

Whitney, however, shook his head. "That third baseman shouldn't have thrown."

When Joey got the ball back he pounded it impatiently into his mitt. He'd made a good pitch and Shorty's piddly hit was a single at best—except for Eric's error.

"It looks like that play rattled him," Whitney told Jason. "He's got to relax and regain his rhythm."

Jason nodded and walked to the on-deck circle.

"Hey, look," the elderly barber said. "The Munson kid is batting third."

"He's certainly earned it," replied the man whose hair he was cutting.

As Jason took his practice swings, he saw Joey walk Wendie Phillips on four straight pitches. Mr. O'Malley called time out and ran to the pitcher's mound.

"It's OK," Jason heard the coach say as he put his arm around Joey. "You got a bad break there. Just throw strikes. Let 'em put the ball in play."

Joey nodded. "OK," he said.

Mr. O'Malley jogged back to the dugout and the ump cried, "Batter up!"

Jason started toward the plate. Before he'd taken three steps, Whitney yelled and motioned him over.

"If I were you," said the bear, "I'd look for the first pitch to be a fastball. He just walked a batter and I'm sure he'll want to throw the easiest pitch to get over."

Jason nodded and stepped out of the dugout. The crowd noise seemed to turn up a notch as he strode toward the plate.

His mother cheered, "Do it Jason!" Dr. Munson chimed in with his usual chorus of "That's my son! That's my son!"

The animals leaned forward.

"Goodness, I'm so tense!" the lioness said.

"My *sss*kin is tingling!" the python confided.

"Come on, Jason!" the piano tuner screamed. "Make it happen!"

Jason stepped into the batter's box, knocked dirt from his cleats, and stared at Joey Flannigan. Joey glanced over his shoulder at the runners and nodded to his catcher.

OK, Jason thought. *Let's see what you've got.*

As if Joey had heard Whitney, he wound up and threw with all his might. The ball came straight over the plate—it didn't curve, it didn't dip, and it certainly didn't sink. No doubt about it: it was the fastball Whitney had predicted. And Jason was ready. He stepped into the ball, and swung. It felt effortless. He heard a crack and took a few steps toward first as the ball took off, deep into left field. Jumping into the air, whooping, he watched the ball disappear over the fence. His first home run.

The crowd exploded. Whitney howled and clapped his paws. What a beginning to his first game ever! He and the other animals began prancing, jumping, and rubbing tails (the animals' answer to the high five).

"Ssstupendousss!" the python cried.

Dr. Munson broke into a second chorus of "That's my son! That's my son!" and hugged his wife as Jason trotted around the bases.

"What a hit!" the judge exclaimed, throwing his Brooklyn Dodger cap into the air. "Jackie Robinson would've been proud!"

"Way to go!" Mr. Handy cried.

Jason was beaming as he crossed the plate. His entire team surrounded him, dispensing high fives and handshakes.

"Nice shot!" Mr. Richardson cried as Jason ran back to the dugout.

Whitney rubbed a paw through Jason's hair.

"Nice swing!"

"Just as you said, it was a fastball."

"And you took it for a ride!"

Mr. O'Malley jogged to the mound.

"Don't worry about it," he said to Joey. "We'll get those runs back. Let's get out of this inning."

But by the time the Highlanders got three out, they'd made another error and the Apaches had scored another run. The score was 4–0 Apaches.

"Your coaching really helped us," Jason told Whitney before he took the field.

"It wasn't my coaching," the bear replied. "It was your homer and the Highlanders' poor fielding."

But the Highlander fans had other opinions.

"That bear distracted our team!" the orthodontist cried.

"That's right!" agreed Mrs. Wiggins. "This game is a sham!"

"Batter up!" the ump shouted, above the complaints.

"No! We insist that you start this game over!" Mrs. Wiggins went on, standing up and striding to the edge of the field. "That bear is giving the Apaches an unfair advantage!"

"Mom!" Homer cried from the Highlander dugout. "Forget it!"

The umpire shook his head. "Listen," he said. "I'll agree that the animals stole the show before the game, but now, I have to admit, they're sitting quietly, enjoying themselves like everyone else. I can't see any harm in it."

"No harm in it?" Mr. Gregory, Annie's father, exclaimed as he joined Mrs. Wiggins. "My daughter's team is behind four to nothing!"

Annie and Homer exchanged glances.

"Sometimes parents can be so embarrassing," she whispered.

"It says nowhere in the rule book that bears can coach!" the orthodontist put in. "And not only that . . . we saw the gnu over there in the dugout before the game. For all we know he gave the Apaches some magical gnu spell!"

"And I think that gorilla did something to the ball!" Mrs. Wiggins whined.

"Come on," Mr. O'Malley called from the dugout. "Enough already."

"The bear stays," the ump said, finally. "Judge Warriner showed me the official papers before the game! Now get back to your seats!"

Suddenly, Mrs. Wiggins, the orthodontist, and Mr. Gregory found themselves surrounded by ten mounted policemen.

112

"Come on," one of the policemen said. "You're holding things up."

The three grown-ups returned, sulking, to their seats. The ump sighed, wishing at that moment he were on a beach in Bermuda getting a good tan.

"Come on!" he yelled. "Batter up! Let's try to finish this game before sunset!"

⑯

"**O**UR boy has quite an arm," Whitney observed to Jason. "Not as powerful as the gorilla perhaps, but I particularly like the way his curve breaks away from left-handed hitters."

Bart was pitching beautifully for the Apaches. His curves curved, his sliders slid, and his fastballs rocketed across the plate. The Highlanders could hardly buy a hit for eight innings.

But Whitney's concern was the Apaches' hitting. He knew hits do not automatically translate into runs. Often, a team gets runners on base but can't come up with that key hit to bring them home. And after a great first inning, rally after rally died with runners on second and third.

Whitney curled his upper lip, thinking. "We've got to get some clutch hits!" he said to Jason after the sixth inning. "Four runs may not hold up. It happened to the Red Sox in the 1986 World Series.

The Mets came from behind in games six and seven to win!"

The bear paced and paced in front of the dugout and finally couldn't resist passing on to Mr. Richardson, through Jason, advice about playing Wendie closer to the third base line. "I'm scared someone's gonna hit it by her for a double."

Mr. Richardson nodded.

For Jason it was a busy afternoon of ball playing and translating, but not so busy he missed seeing how much fun his friend was having.

And the gnu, too. He became the team's most ardent cheerleader. Every time an Apache got a hit he pranced up and down the first base line, crying to Jason, "Ripping good! Smashing! Abraham Lincoln would be so proud!"

The reporters had a field day snapping pictures of the gorilla working on his famous "windmill windup" over behind third.

The lioness, Jason noticed with a smile, spent much of the afternoon thrilled for the team, but nonetheless squatting behind Mr. Handy with her jaw firmly shut for safety's sake.

But even Jason lost track of the python, who observed one inning from a policeman's horse (directly behind the officer) and another from atop the fence in left field.

By the bottom of the ninth, confident Apache fans were getting ready to rush the field and savor a

4–0 shutout. The Highlanders were up for their last licks.

"It's not over until it's over!" Mrs. Wiggins cried as the Apaches took the field.

"Little rally!" the orthodontist shouted. "Little rally!"

"A few longballs and we're right back in it," the sergeant observed.

"OK," Mr. O'Malley told his team in the dugout. "We're only behind by four runs. The meat of our order is up! We've got them right where we want them!"

After receiving high fives from everyone on his team, the first Highlander batter walked into the on-deck circle. In the Apache dugout, a beaming coach Richardson said to Whitney: "We're in, I tell you. This game is just about wrapped up!"

Whitney smiled, but inside he was worried. In the eighth inning, Bart had begun to look tired. He'd given up solid hits to the two weakest Highlander hitters and had only squeaked out of the inning when Shorty Rodgers turned a sure base hit into a double play. The question for Whitney was: could Bart's arm last for three more outs?

Bart knew he was tired. He knew he had to pour all his available strength into every pitch. He couldn't let up—not now—not after the best game of his career. Grimly determined, he faced the first batter.

116

It was Bobby Windmeyer. Bart wound up and threw a fastball. Bobby swung and hit an easy grounder to shortstop. Shorty threw him out.

"One down!" the umpire said.

"Brilliant!" the gnu cried.

"Come on, Apaches!" Mrs. Munson cried. "Let's sew it up!"

"This is certainly going to be a cherished childhood memory for these boys and girls," Dr. Munson declared cheerfully.

"What'd I tell you?" Mr. Richardson chirped to Whitney. "We're in! We're in!"

Whitney nodded. That pitch Bart had thrown looked surprisingly good. And then he proceeded to strike out the next batter on three straight pitches. The Apache bench went crazy.

"They're making it happen," the piano tuner observed. "It's happening like it's never happened before!"

But the more diehard Highlander fans weren't giving up.

"Come on!" Mrs. Wiggins shrieked. "We've still got one more out!"

Next up was Annie Gregory, a good contact hitter. She had grounded out twice and singled.

Bart wound up and threw the ball as hard as he could. Annie swung evenly and lined a hard single to center field.

"Oh no," the gnu said to Whitney. "Is that bad?"

Whitney shook his head. "Nah," he said. "He shouldn't have thrown the heater, but it's not tragic."

Wyatt Torple threw to Jason who ran the ball over to Bart.

"Don't worry about it," he said. "Just get this next guy."

Bart nodded, punched the ball into his mitt, and faced the catcher. The batter was Ray Thomas. The crowd was on its feet, its cheers echoing in Bart's ears.

"Blow it by him!"

"He's no hitter!"

"The pitcher stinks!"

Bart wound up and threw another fastball—a mistake, because he was getting tired. The ball came straight over the plate and Ray stroked it into left field. Runners on first and second. Jason looked toward the dugout and exchanged a glance with Whitney. The bear shook his head solemnly. He knew Bart's fastball had lost its pop.

Eric Hadden, one of the Highlanders' best hitters, stepped up to the plate, hoping to make up with his bat for his first inning error.

"Come on!" Eric's father yelled.

"They're tryin' to nickel and dime 'em," the hot dog man said. "I only hope they're startin' too late!"

His hand raised, Mr. Richardson jogged to the

mound. The umpire called time. Jason and the rest of the infielders gathered around.

"How do you feel?" the coach asked.

"OK," Bart said. "A little beat, but I'm hanging in there."

"All right, but remember—science teaches us that . . ."

◊ WHITNEY LICKED his lips as Mr. Richardson trotted toward him in the dugout. He hoped the coach had given Bart the right tip, to stick with sliders. Bart checked the runners and threw home. Another mistake; another fastball . . .

"No!" Whitney groaned. "Not again!"

Eric swung. The ball rocketed into the right field corner. Jim Lanier turned and began running as fast as his slow legs would allow. The crowd went wild. Annie Gregory scored; Ray Thomas was rounding third and heading for home. The ball hit the ground and rolled to the wall. Jim, who was pouring it on, still had twenty feet to go.

"All right!" Mrs. Wiggins screamed.

"Oh, dear!" said the lioness.

It looked like an easy double.

But then something incredible happened.

When Jim Lanier was still ten feet from the ball, what looked like a giant whip wrapped around it and lashed through the air. In a flash, the ball had flown straight home into the mitt of the surprised catcher Judy Wheeler. Ray slowed, skidded, and slipped awkwardly right into Judy's glove.

"You're out!" the umpire cried, going down on one knee and signaling with his thumb.

It had happened so fast, half the Apache fans were unaware that Jim hadn't fielded the ball. But the Highlander fans realized it. They screamed bloody murder.

"Cheat!"

"No!"

And Jason—he knew.

Immediately after the play he ran to right field.

"Hey, python!" he cried.

"Greetingsss!" the python said with a mischievous laugh. "Pretty nice tosss, huh?"

"Yeah," Jason said. "What are you doing out here?"

"Jussst getting a better view," the snake said.

Soon, the umpire realized what had happened. Once he did, he looked up to see—to his horror— a giant mass that could only have been Mrs. Wiggins storming toward him. Behind him came the orthodontist and a whole slew of Highlander parents. He looked above him toward the heavens.

"Why me?" he murmured. "Why me?"

By then everyone knew who had thrown out Ray Thomas.

"The Apaches are cheating!" Mrs. Wiggins shrieked.

Jason's parents and Judge Warriner rushed onto the field.

"Count all three runs!" the orthodontist fumed.

"Three?" the umpire said. "But Eric wouldn't have scored even if the snake wasn't in the outfield!"

"How do you know?" Mrs. Wiggins cut in. "Eric is a very fast boy and that right fielder might have dropped the ball!"

An uproar ensued. Highlander fans against Apache fans; Coach Richardson arguing with Coach O'Malley, the Munsons with Mrs. Wiggins. Only the umpire wasn't arguing. He spent the time dreaming about a hot bubble bath.

Finally, Jason ran in from right field.

"Hold it!" he said. "Hold it!"

"What?" Mrs. Wiggins said.

"Give them the three runs."

"What?" Dr. Munson exclaimed.

"They can have 'em, Dad," Jason said. "It doesn't make any difference. We're gonna win anyway!"

That settled it. The fielders took their positions. The scoreboard was changed to read 4–3 and two outs. The python slithered off the field, chuckling to himself.

"Well, I hope you're satisfied, the gnu said."

"Oh yesss," the python replied. "I ssshowed them what a real play at the plate can be."

"OK," Mr. Richardson told Bart. "Just get this next guy and we can all go home!"

17

B<small>UT</small> the next batter, Nick Hanning, lined a single to right. Then Nina Spine ripped a double into the gap in left-center. Highlander fans whooped, Apache fans moaned. There were runners on second and third. A hit would win the game. In the dugout, Mr. Richardson put a hand over his eyes.

"Bart's been doing it for us all year! I can't take him out now!"

Whitney was doing some quick, serious thinking. Next up for the Highlanders was Homer Wiggins. If Bart threw another weak fastball it was all over.

"Certainly looks grim," the gnu said.

The bear made a decision. Slowly, he shook himself out of the seat he'd been in for the past eight innings, stepped from the dugout, and lumbered toward the pitcher's mound. Everyone gasped.

"It's the bear! It's the bear!"

"I know! I can see!"

"That's him! The genius behind the Apaches!"

It took three mounted policemen to keep the reporters from storming the field.

"Come on!" one cried. "Gimme an interview."

"Let me hear what's going on!" another said. "The public has a right to know!"

Everyone wanted to know what Whitney would say. Mrs. Wiggins, however, was more outraged than curious.

"That bear is going to hex my son!" she bellowed.

The umpire turned around, exasperated.

"Listen, lady," he declared. "You're giving me a headache! You act like you never saw a polar bear walk to the pitcher's mound before!"

Mrs. Wiggins tried to speak, but, for once, couldn't find the words.

As Whitney made his slow, steady way across the infield, Judy Wheeler joined Bart and Jason on the mound.

"Hi," Bart said as Whitney drew up.

Whitney nodded and looked at Jason.

"Listen," he said. "Tell him to forget about his fastball. He's too tired. Tell him to throw nothing but sliders. It's his only pitch that's still got any bite to it."

With those words, Whitney turned and made his way back to the dugout.

"What'd he say?" Bart asked.

Jason repeated the message word for word. Bart thought about it, nodded.

"Listen," Jason said to Judy. "Flash some fake signs to confuse Homer. He doesn't have to know we're going with the same pitch."

"Good idea," she said. "No matter what sign I give you, throw the slider."

Judy jogged back to the plate and Jason took his position at second.

"Batter up!" the umpire said.

Homer Wiggins walked toward the plate.

"Come on!" a Highlander fan cried. "Live up to your name, Homer!"

"Hit one! Do it!" cried another.

"Dial eight!"

"Hit a dinger!"

"Go downtown, baby!"

"Do the four-sack mamba!"

Whitney hunched anxiously at the edge of the dugout. The other animals pranced and jumped. Mr. Richardson was pacing back and forth.

"Let's go!" he cried.

Homer rubbed dirt on his hands and stepped up to the plate. Bart stared at him. Judy flashed a sign. Bart shook his head. Judy flashed another. This time Bart nodded.

"Come on, Homer!" Mrs. Wiggins cried. "Make your mother proud!"

Bart threw home. The pitch did what all good

sliders must do to earn their name—came straight across the plate and at the last second slid sharply toward Homer's wrists. Homer swung and missed.

"Strike one!" the umpire cried.

The crowd stirred.

"All right!"

"Fan him!"

Homer took a deep breath and stepped out of the box. That pitch had fooled him. On the sidelines, Whitney nodded gravely at Bart. He knew that relying only on sliders was risky.

Once again, Judy flashed Bart some fake signs to confuse Homer. Homer stepped back into the box. Nina Spine took a lead off second. Nick Hanning was ready to sprint home from third. Jason felt his stomach tighten. Bart wound up and threw.

"OK," Homer thought. "This is the one."

He brought the bat off his shoulder and swung with all his might. But again the ball slid at the last minute and instead of whacking it, Homer merely fouled it back against the backstop.

"Strike two!" the ump called.

The crowd noise doubled. Jason shot a glance at Whitney. To Jason, his friend looked as calm as day—almost serene. But Whitney was as nervous as anyone, his great chest feeling suddenly too small for the pounding of his heart.

Bart got the ball back again. The atmosphere was charged. Mrs. Wiggins's fists were clenched. Judge Warriner pulled at the sides of his Brooklyn Dodgers cap. Dr. and Mrs. Munson were holding each other. Whitney crossed his claws for luck, hoping Homer hadn't realized that Bart was too tired to throw any of his other pitches well—because if Homer was expecting another slider, he would hit it a mile.

Homer took his place in the batter's box. The umpire crouched down. Bart shook off some signs. Judy put out her mitt as a target. There followed a moment when everyone was quiet and everything was still. Then, channeling every last bit of strength into the pitch, he wound up, looked over his shoulder at the runner, and threw home. Whitney stood up on all fours.

Jason experienced the next few seconds as though in slow motion. He saw Homer lunge and the ball spin off his bat toward shallow right. Jason snapped around. Jim Lanier was playing far too deep and was far too slow to get it. Unless Jason caught the ball, it would drop in for a base hit—both runs would score and the Highlanders would win. Reacting quickly, he turned and ran straight back toward the right-field fence, glove outstretched. He heard muted cheers and saw the crowd rise. Homer Wiggins flew toward first. Nick Hanning sped home, Nina Spine following close behind. The gnu pranced down the line. The python slithered up the gorilla's shoulders to get a better view.

"Jason ball!" cried the gorilla. "Jason ball!"

"Oh, dear!" the lioness pleaded. "Catch it!"

The ball reached the top of its arc and began to

126

drop. Jason couldn't afford a split second to try looking for it. He had to run all out. His cleats dug into
the outfield grass. He could hear himself panting.
Finally, he took a mighty leap forward and dove,
his glove out in front of him. He heard a plunk. He
rolled over onto his back and pulled his mitt toward
his chest. Jim Lanier ran up next to him.

"He caught it!" Jim cried. "He caught it!"

Jason stood up and held his mitt high in the air.

"Out!" the umpire cried.

Jason let out a whoop and threw his arms around
Jim. In an instant, they were surrounded by the rest
of the team. Mr. Richardson tore out of the dugout.
The crowd poured onto the field.

"Ripping good!" the gnu cried, dancing onto the
field.

"Jason catchy!" the gorilla boomed. "Jason
catchy!"

"Wonderful!" the lioness yelled.

"Sssnagged it!" the python shouted, dropping off
the gorilla's back.

Apache players slapped backs and threw their
caps in the air.

"Terrific job!" Judge Warriner beamed. "This was
as good as the '55 Series!"

"I'm so proud of you," Mrs. Munson said.

"Here's my son!" Dr. Munson cried. "This one!
The fellow who caught the ball!"

Whitney was happier than he'd ever been—
including the day he'd first heard a game on the

radio. At the sight of Jason's catch, he jumped in the air and began to charge the field.

But before he took more than a few steps he felt a sharp pain in his chest. He stopped short and then sprawled onto the bench, breathing heavily.

No one, including Jason, noticed.

"Ya nickel and dimed 'em," the hot dog man said, shaking Jason's hand. "Congratulations!"

"Cheers! Cheers!" Mr. Richardson yelled.

The teams broke into two separate groups and cheered for their opponents. The piano tuner shook Jason's hand. The barber offered him a free haircut and Miss Martin kissed him on the cheek. Then, all of a sudden, Homer Wiggins was standing before him. Behind him were Mrs. Wiggins and Mr. O'Malley.

"Good game," Homer said.

"Thanks," Jason said. "You too."

"You've got a fine career ahead of you, son," Mr. O'Malley added.

"Thank you," Jason said.

"Your son is quite a ballplayer," Dr. Munson told Mrs. Wiggins.

"I know," Mrs. Wiggins replied. "I'm very proud of him. But I still say the Highlanders would have won if it wasn't for that . . ."

Homer shot his mother a glance.

"Well," Mrs. Wiggins ended, with a smile, "I have to admit it—that bear is something special."

Jason smiled.

"Hey," Dr. Munson said. "Where is Whitney anyway?"

"Yeah," a reporter cried. "I want an interview!"

Everyone looked around. Then, out of the corner of his eye, Jason saw Mr. Handy and the sergeant scramble into the dugout. Jason's face turned white. Something was wrong.

He sprinted toward them, dodging people on his way.

"Jason!" his mother cried.

It wasn't until he was close that he saw Whitney.

"Stay away, son," the sergeant said, holding Jason back.

Jason squirmed free and knelt next to his friend. Whitney was lying on his side on the dugout bench. Mr. Handy was sitting next to him, the bear's head on his lap. Whitney's eyes were half closed. His breathing was labored. Jason took his paw.

The great bear looked up. "Nice catch," he said weakly.

Jason swallowed hard.

"What happened?"

"Just a little chest pain," Whitney said. "It's nothing."

A crowd formed quickly around the dugout. The other animals, Jason's parents, and the judge pushed close. Just then, an ambulance pulled into the parking lot. Three men got out, carrying a stretcher.

"Clear the way!" the sergeant yelled. "Clear the way!"

The crowd shifted, opening an aisle to the dugout. The men hustled through. Everyone was silent as they rolled Whitney onto the stretcher.

"Chin up, Whitney," the gnu called out.

Jason jogged along beside the stretcher. Whitney's eyes were shut now. Jason couldn't believe what was happening. A second ago he had made the game-winning catch. . . . Though he was vaguely aware of his parents, the animals, and the judge walking beside him, all his thoughts were for his stricken friend. He wanted to say something, but before he could think of what, Whitney was being lifted into the back of the ambulance.

"Whitney, I . . ." Jason began.

The doors shut with a loud bang before he could finish. The siren blared and the ambulance lurched away from the field.

(18)

Later that afternoon, Jason met Mr. Handy at the zoo. "Glad you could make it," the zookeeper said.

"How is he?" Jason asked.

Mr. Handy's face clouded over. "He's been better. But he's a tough old bear. Seeing you will cheer him up."

He and Jason walked up the hill and turned the corner into the courtyard. The animals were all back in their cages.

"Jason!" the gorilla boomed.

"Hello there," the gnu said.

"How's*sss* the hero?"

"OK," Jason said.

"Going to see Whitney?" the lioness asked. Jason nodded.

"He'll appreciate that," the gnu said.

Mr. Handy unlocked Whitney's cage and pushed open the gate.

"I'd better go," Jason said.

"That's right, dear," the lioness replied.

"See you all soon."

Jason slipped into the cage and walked silently by the swimming hole, up the rocks, and into the cave. It felt strange to make the short journey without Whitney's tail to grab hold of. He walked slowly, feeling the rock walls with his palms. He ducked and turned right. After a few long steps, he was inside. Whitney was lying to his left, hunched over a stack of clippings.

"Glad you could make it," he said. "Have a seat."

Jason sat on a stack of paper and looked around. The room looked pretty much the same as it had on his visit two weeks earlier. Without speaking, Whitney reached slowly for an article, and, concentrating hard, folded it and placed it on a pile. When he was done, he reached for another.

"What are you doing?" Jason asked.

"Oh, just getting things a little more organized."

"Organized?" Jason asked. "For what?"

Whitney kept folding silently. When he finally spoke, his tone was very matter of fact.

"So it's easier for you to take back to your apartment after I'm gone."

Jason sat up.

"What?" he said. "What?"

There was a silence. Whitney stared straight at Jason. Jason could see that his friend's eyes were very tired and his face looked suddenly thin.

"When you get to be my age," Whitney said softly, "it's either one thing or another. I'm so weak now I could barely lift my paw to show you how to hit a curveball."

"What are you telling me?" Jason asked.

"Only that I'm an old bear," Whitney said. "Very old. I'm not going to be around much longer."

"It isn't true!"

Whitney shook his head. "I'm afraid it's very true."

"But at the ball game you said it was nothing."

"That's what I hoped," the bear replied.

"How much longer?"

"Not much."

Jason was shocked. Even after that afternoon's game, it hadn't occurred to him that this could be the end. They had too much left to talk about. Jason looked at his friend—for the first time he noticed Whitney's ribs. He started crying.

"But who am I going to talk about baseball with? Who's going to help me next year?"

Whitney raised his left paw.

"Slow down a minute," he said. "You aren't some little substitute now. You're the star of the team. You don't need me anymore. You have Bart and plenty of other friends to talk with. And if you do need a little help here and there, Mr. Richardson'll show you."

"It's the game today that made you sick," Jason

stammered. "I never should have arranged for you to go to the game."

Whitney grabbed Jason by the shoulders.

"That's ridiculous and you know it! Don't say dumb things like that! It makes me uncomfortable!" Then he continued more gently, easing his arms back down onto the floor of the cave. "I know it's sudden, but I've lived through lots of seasons and I've had a good, long life. Why I was alive when Roger Maris hit sixty-one homers! And when Don Larsen pitched his perfect game in the 1956 World Series. . . ."

Jason was silent.

"You can start moving my stuff out tomorrow if you like," Whitney said. "I'm sure not going to need all this when I'm dead. And the next polar bear they get in here may not be a baseball fan or appreciate a cluttered cave."

"But I'd feel funny. They're your—"

Before Jason could finish, Whitney reached out with his big arms, pulled Jason toward him, and hugged him tight. Jason buried his face deep in Whitney's fur.

"Take my things," Whitney said, after another heavy silence. "Then I'll know they'll be in good hands."

Jason nodded, his head still pressed into Whitney's chest.

"Was that a yes?" the bear asked.

Jason pulled himself free and sat down across from Whitney.

"Yes."

"Good," Whitney said. "Now, try and get this: Who played shortstop for the 1924 Washington Senators and what was his batting average?"

Jason leaned forward. Though Whitney's face had gone thin, his eyes hadn't lost their spark.

"You must be referring to Roger Peckinpaugh."

"Right!" Whitney said. "And his average?"

"Oh . . . let's see," Jason said. ".285?"

"Almost," Whitney laughed. "You're a little high. It was .272. Now, see if you get this one," the bear continued. "Who played left field for that same team?"

"Easy!" Jason cried. "Goose Goslin!"

"Right-o!" Whitney said. "Old Goose Goslin. A fine batter because he knew how to hit the breaking ball. He hit .344 that year. He's in the Hall of Fame. I think at one point in his career he had a thirty-game hit streak."

"Not bad," Jason said.

"You're right it's not bad. Not as good as Joe DiMaggio, who got a hit in fifty-six straight games in 1941, but still pretty presentable."

"Hey, Whitney?"

"Yes?"

"Why do you think DiMaggio won the MVP that year when Ted Williams hit over .400?"

Whitney chuckled. "That's a question that's been occupying baseball experts ever since," he said. "It certainly was a tough choice that year."

The boy and the bear talked about baseball for another half hour. Before they knew it, Mr. Handy was shouting:

"Jason! Sorry, but Whitney needs his rest."

The bear, who had been telling Jason about Carl Yastrzemski's early years on the Boston Red Sox, stopped mid-sentence.

"So," he sighed. "I guess that's it. It's just as well. I am tired. You'd better get going."

"Yeah," Jason said. "You can finish the story tomorrow."

"Right," Whitney said. "Tomorrow."

Jason rubbed his hand over Whitney's head and then, suddenly, did something he had never done before—he leaned forward and kissed him on the cheek.

"Thanks for the stuff," Jason whispered. "I'll take good care of it."

Whitney nodded.

"Good," he said. "I'll rest easier tonight knowing that."

"Take care," Jason said. "See you tomorrow."

"Good," Whitney said. "Good."

" 'Bye!"

"So long, pal. So long."

19

THE next day, the city's morning paper carried this story on the front page:

BASEBALL BEAR DIES

One of the city's finest citizens, Whitney the polar bear, died at the zoo last night. Though Whitney only came to the sporting public's attention recently, he created a sensation, helping coach the Little League Apaches to a championship.

The elderly bear was stricken after the final game of that series. He was returned to his cave late last afternoon and late last night his body was discovered by Mr. George Handy, the zookeeper.

According to Handy, the bear was lying peacefully in a corner of his cave. A true fan to the last, the bear had before him a baseball encyclopedia open to a page of statistics on the 1924 Washington Senators. An article dated June 12, 1957, about Ted Williams was spread open to his right. Cradled in the bear's right paw was what Handy called Whitney's most prized possession—a baseball that Jason Munson, a fourth grader on the Apache team, had given him two weeks earlier.

"Jason was Whitney's best friend," Handy said. "That ball meant a lot to the bear."

Jason Munson is widely regarded as the first human to talk successfully to animals outside of stories. He could not be reached for comment.

"The city has lost a true friend," the mayor said by telephone late last night.

Whitney will be buried tomorrow at the Animal Cemetery on Grove Street. Instead of flowers, Handy suggested that gifts to the city's Youth Athletics Fund would be appropriate.

20

"THE loss of a loved one," Dr. Munson explained to Jason the night after Whitney died, "is always traumatic. One often has conflicting emotions—anger, sadness, despair. . . . It takes time to come to terms with these feelings."

Every day after school, Jason walked home through the zoo and took a moment to stare into Whitney's cage. He felt like part of him had been stripped away.

"He was a fine chap," the gnu said sadly one day. "He was worthy of a Shakespeare sonnet. No—if Shakespeare were alive I dare say he'd write a play about him."

Jason nodded, knowing what a high compliment that was from the likes of the gnu.

"That'*sss* correct," the python agreed. "Whitney wa*sss* the true king of all animal*sss.*"

"Remember, dear," the lioness said. "You always have his memory."

"Whitney kind," the gorilla observed. "Whitney very, very kind!"

The first week or so after Whitney's death, Jason spent most of his time in his room with Bart, sorting through the bear's clipping collection.

"Joe DiMaggio!" Jason would say, imitating Whitney. "Now there was a hitter! Look at the way he's stepping into the pitch with his left leg. And how about this picture of Don Drysdale—what a fast-ball!"

Every week Jason took a bus to the edge of the city to the animal cemetery to put one of the clippings on Whitney's grave.

After a month, when he was feeling a little better, Jason agreed to an interview on a local news program.

"Whitney was a tough coach," Jason said. "But always kind."

"And what do you plan to do with all the clippings he left you?"

"Well," Jason said. "I've decided to give them to the Hall of Fame."

The next day it was done. The museum set up a special exhibit of Whitney's collection.

◊ IN LATE February the papers began to carry news of baseball teams heading to Florida and Arizona for spring training. And then, in early April at the first Apache practice, Jason showed he hadn't lost his touch with the bat.

140

"Those Highlanders had better start sweating," Mr. Richardson chuckled that afternoon.

The season began. Every day Jason went to the zoo to keep his old friends up to date on the team's progress. The gnu became an expert statistician. He kept long charts mathematically documenting every aspect of Jason's game.

"Look here!" he said one day, a month into the season. "You're hitting .450 with runners in scoring position! And your on-base percentage is an impressive .525!"

"Jason star!" the gorilla cheered.

"Does your sssquad need any more outfield-ersss?" the python asked with a grin.

One Tuesday in mid-July Jason stopped by the zoo just after a game. As usual he walked straight to the gnu's cage to tell him how he'd done that day, so he could bring Jason's stats up to date. But as Jason passed Whitney's old cage, he saw a flash of white! He stopped in his tracks. His heart jumped. Was his mind playing tricks on him or had something just moved?

Jason crept to the side of the cage. Plodding out of the shadows was a polar bear! This bear was obviously much younger than Whitney; he was sleek and his fur showed few creases.

"Hey!" Jason said.

The other animals laughed.

"Isn't he a dear?" the lioness said.

"Wow!" Jason exclaimed. "What's his name?"

"Charlie! Charlie! Charlie!" the gorilla cried.

Jason turned to the cage. The polar bear walked to the edge and stuck his nose between the bars.

"Hi, Charlie," Jason said.

Charlie moved his lips. All Jason heard was a friendly growl. Jason turned to the other animals.

"Hey! Did he just say something?"

"Of course," the gnu said. "He said, 'Hello.' "

"Didn't you hear?" the lioness asked.

"No," Jason said.

He tried again. "Do you want to learn about baseball?"

Again the polar bear moved his lips in Jason's direction.

"I'm losing my hearing or something," Jason said, looking to the other animals for help. "I can't make out the words. What did he say?"

"He said, 'Baseball? What's baseball?' " the gnu explained.

"Why didn't I understand him?" Jason looked alarmed.

The gnu shrugged. "I couldn't say. But don't be angry. It appears you can still understand us. We'll translate for Charlie."

Jason agreed. And by the end of the Little League season, with the other animals translating, Charlie had become an avid baseball fan. The season passed quickly and once again the Apaches faced the Highlanders for the championship.

Before the first play-off game the mayor and all

142

of his commissioners gathered at the ballfield for a special ceremony. Everyone Jason knew was there —his parents, his teammates, his friends, his teachers, Judge Warriner, the hot dog man, the sergeant, the orthodontist, the piano tuner, the barber, and, of course, the animals. Before them was an eight-foot-tall structure, wrapped with a large white sheet.

"This statue is in honor of one of the city's finest citizens and baseball fans ever!" the mayor said in his dedication.

Then two parks workers pulled the white sheet off the statue. The crowd took a deep breath.

"It's beautiful!" Mrs. Munson said.

The statue was simple, yet elegant—done in white marble. Whitney was standing on his hind legs, a mitt on one paw and a ball in the other. Below the statue in bold lettering was a plaque that read: WHITNEY—THE BASEBALL BEAR.

Everyone clapped. The mayor shook Jason's hand. The children petted the animals, even the python. After a short time, the spectators took their seats and the players went off to warm up on the sidelines.

Jason, the last to leave, took another look at the statue. He stared at Whitney's long, thin face, pointing straight ahead. He moved his eyes down to the bear's broad shoulders and then further down the marble to Whitney's right paw, holding on proudly to a baseball.

It occurred to him, as if for the first time, that he had been taught how to hit by a polar bear—not many other kids are lucky enough to say that.

"Come on!" Bart yelled. "We're up first!"

Jason took a final look at the statue and, smiling, sprinted to the Apache dugout.

"Play ball!" the ump cried.

ABOUT THE AUTHOR

DAN ELISH is the author of *The World-wide Dessert Contest*, a Bantam Skylark book, and *The Great Squirrel Uprising*. He lives in New York City.

Wild and crazy adventures from
Stephen Manes!

☐ **BE A PERFECT PERSON IN
JUST THREE DAYS!**   15580-6 $3.25

Milo Crinkley tries to follow the loony instructions on being
perfect, found in a library book. But who ever heard of wearing
a stalk of broccoli around your neck for twenty-four hours? And
that's only the first day...

☐ **IT'S NEW! IT'S IMPROVED!
IT'S TERRIBLE!**   15682-9 $2.99

The TV commercials say the shoes that basketball star Ralph
"Helicopter" Jones wears are "New! IMPROVED! Amazing!
NEAT!" Arnold Schlemp just has to have them. At least until
the commercial steps out of his TV set and into his life!

☐ **CHICKEN TREK**   15716-7 $2.99

Oscar Noodleman spends his summer vacation entering the
"Chicken in the Bag" contest and eating 211 chicken meals at
restaurants across America! But Oscar's not the only one after
the $99,999.99 prize. Join the Chicken Trek!